What happens when a 20th century human being awakens suddenly to a vast panorama of Earth and beyond? Zooming into the next century to witness a monumental shift of human and animal consciousness, be prepared to do a few double takes with this human — as the greater galaxies unfold.

When the fable's human protagonist is not conveying to the reader thoughts about the extraordinary scenes witnessed, he/she is engaging in a dialogue with a myriad of beings from the greater galactic arena.

The human slowly grows in understanding and wisdom as a result of these interactions, and the ability to see past, present and future in what might be called a virtual reality:

". . . suddenly I — oh my — am light as a feather in the wind. . . . I have . . . wings. How exhilarating to smell and taste the sweetness inside this flower . . . feeling the warmth of sun and the smell of Earth. . . . can you feel the wings? . . . and the wind helps me float . . . feel the wings. . . ."

At the heart of the book's messages is this: "And it is through the concept of All Things Great and Small that there exists a God spoken soul contract between animals and humans, such that Earth's evolvement depends on a shared bond of healing. . . ."

ONE
SPIRALLING
DANCE

Joan Haywood Helene

To Kay with love and gratitude
for your outreach and
generosity of soul!!
Keep being!
- Joan

17 Rainier Ct.
Hackettstown NJ 07840

jghhel@aol.com

ONE
SPIRALLING
DANCE

A Fable of
All Things
Great and Small

THE TRIAD

Canadian Cataloguing in Publication Data

Triad.
  One spiralling dance

  ISBN 1-55212-285-9

  I. Title.
PS3570.R49O5 1999   813'.54   C99-911094-2

TRAFFORD

This book was published *on-demand* in cooperation with Trafford Publishing.
On-demand publishing is a unique process and service of making a book available for retail sale to the public taking advantage of on-demand manufacturing and Internet marketing.
On-demand publishing includes promotions, retail sales, manufacturing, order fulfilment, accounting and collecting royalties on behalf of the author.

Suite 6E - 2333 Government St., Victoria, BC, Canada V8T 4P4

Phone	250-383-6864	Toll-free	1-888-232-4444 (Canada & US)
Fax	250-383-6804	E-mail	sales@trafford.com
Web site	www.trafford.com	TRAFFORD PUBLISHING IS A DIVISION OF TRAFFORD HOLDINGS LTD.
Trafford Catalogue #99-0036		www.trafford.com/robots/99-0036.html	

10   9   8   7   6   5   4

All three of us wish to express our immense gratitude to Susan Fossett for her wonderful technical assistance and hard work; to Kerry Canfield of Precision Graphics in Black Mountain, NC for much patience with color scanning; to Brandon and Nate for their enthusiastic and creative manifestation of the ideas for the book's cover and inside illustrations — quite an accomplishment for high school students; to Lisa Guglielmi and Tanis Toope of Trafford for guiding us smoothly through the publishing process; and to Greg Heleine for his computer knowledge and assistance. Everything would have been so much more difficult and tedious but for all of you —THANKS!!!

✳ ✳ ✳

"Magic Words" from MAGIC WORDS, copyright © 1968, 1967 by Edward Field, reprinted by permission of Harcourt, Inc.

Excerpt from "The Ghost Continent" THE UNEXPECTED UNIVERSE, copyright © 1969 by Loren Eiseley and renewed 1997 by John A. Eichman, III, reprinted by permission of Harcourt, Inc.

Permission to reprint from *The Gospel of the Holy Twelve* by S. G. J. Ouseley graciously provided by Health Research, P.O. Box 850, Pomeroy, WA 99347; 1-888-844-2386; www.healthresearchbooks.com.

The triad is incredibly grateful and in awe of Those we list herein, for their LOVE, GUIDANCE, INSTIGATION AND INSPIRATION for this work:

GOD/GODDESS, Creator of All

Christ Consciousness

Mary

Triadic Event Consciousness

Dale, Taylor and Valor

All Things Great and Small On High

Sirian Sisterhood: Altiria, Eleanor, Elowis, Kopqut, Querin, Rustinor, Ruwnor, Squomor, Tamor, Wopjne

Arcturian Sisterhood: Rophik, Tronpos, Viminor

North Star Sisterhood: Gorgon, Rontux, Tedstre

Pleiadian Sisterhood: Stylmas, Tophez, Vonort

Angelic Presences: Eleanor, Gosin, Mopsut, Taos, Valor, Grenadear

Archangel Michael

The White Brotherhood

Daleian Connection On High

Crystalline Structures On High: Harstal, Lathur, Tamor

Ronar, The Magnificent — and Friends

The E.T.s

The Hopi Great Elders On High

The I-Ching

The Akashics of Old — as They Emanate into The Higher Records

Children's Network On High

DEDICATION

It is a true blessing in this life to have not only a loving family, partner, and companion dog, but also incredible friends — not to mention all the remarkable animals who have crossed my path. I thank you all for your unconditional love. You know who you are.

MAG

I am thankful for the gifts that I receive daily from family, friends and my companion cat — and feel special gratitude for and connection with my true son, The Great Elder Spirit, Kim Sung Hoon.

JHH

Blessings and thanksgiving to my family and friends, especially my loving husband. My life is ever richer because of you — and our ever expanding family of cats.

MFH

CONTENTS

Introduction xiii

The Fable 1

True Beginnings 5

All Things Great And Small 9

Elevation To Animals On High 27

Evolving Descent Into Manifestation 37

Planetary Movers Speak 43

Deeper Into Matter 57

Higher Into Manifestation 63

Third Dimensional Illusion of Separateness 75

Cost Of Separateness 85

Handicapping Of Communication 95

Interconnectedness Of All Things 107

Direct Connection With Shamanic Essence 115

Magnificent Shifts 121

Structural Integration . . . And New Heights 163

Into The Garden 169

Glossary 179

Endnotes 202

INTRODUCTION

Prior to emerging into 3rd Dimensional Earth (in February 1943, October 1943, and June 1945, respectively) we make a contract to meet here and subsequently embark on a joint mission. Up until the summer of 1997 this is consciously unknown to any of us. We have no other explanation.

Growing up in different states, in very different ways, we wind up doing various forms of human services work: combinations of therapy/counseling, social work, teaching. Over several years beginning in 1979, our paths begin to cross, two at a time.

In June, 1997, we all three meet together for the first time. At this point in our mid lives, each of us has individually experienced a spiritual reawakening: one at the

Wailing Wall in Jerusalem, one after several intensive workshops related to energy work, and one through the initiation of past-life therapies. At this initial meeting THEY inform us we are "the triad" — and indeed have signed on for a specific mission. Each month thereafter, we sit looking at each other, attempting to comprehend the magnitude of what is happening.

Did we really make a contract to do this? We ask THEM if we have shared other lifetimes and the answer is "yes," but are told that in these settings we were unable to fulfill a spiritual mission because we were not connected enough to stay with the work. With <u>that</u> information we can only hope for a reprieve this time around! *"Validate that the three of you took this 'work' from within the Interlife as your mission for this lifetime, and you took the vow together to seek each other at the appropriate time to do this work on Earth."*

Oh.

". . . But you were not aware of the density on Earth and the veil which would cover your eyes, so you would not remember the truth of God On High." We imagine that we're not the only ones who have questioned the wisdom of re-entering this veiled dimension.

Looking back over the past two years, we realize the BEINGS have always been on target, though it is sometimes difficult to hear the truth. On the other hand, the amount of humor/laughter which penetrates our gatherings is amazing, as well as therapeutic. It pours out especially when we find ourselves, as we dub it, "digressing away from the subject at hand." The latest message: *"You have now surpassed your record for digression into eternity."*

Whenever we doubt ourselves, messages come through which surely speak to all living things everywhere: *"The truth is that each of you is so much more than you can encompass, it does boggle the mind."*

Initially, as we mentioned, THEY refer to us as the triad, and our monthly sessions as "triadic events." Later, the events become triadic "occasions" and, recently, triadic "happenings."

During one particular "event", someone remembers that, even as a child there existed a vague "knowing" that something bigger than herself would unfold much later, so it never really occurred to her to establish what one would call a career goal. When the other two think back, one recognizes that even at age six, she wondered about her true purpose in life. The other remembers that as a young child she felt connected with something greater than linear reality.

Perhaps you are now wondering what all this has to do with the book you are about to read. A relatively brief chronology may help put things in perspective.

On June 14, 1997, our first meeting together, Joan finds herself doing some automatic writing (much to her surprise!) — not knowing what might transpire. Maxine and Maria take turns noting everything verbatim. To date, the sum total comes to over 700 pages, including our own bizarre shorthand.

As if to set the tone for what is to come, one of the first notes reads: *"This is the start of something big, and it will mean significant changes in your lives. We are in this together for the duration."* The next day's session only confirms our amazement: *"What has happened is that you are now in touch with another dimension."*

Oh, again.

Who are THEY? Our collective Higher Selves called (by THEM) YEOMEN, numbers 350 at this time. What is all this really about? *"There is work for all of you and of the highest order . . . not to be taken lightly."* We of course need something more concrete, being our 3rd Dimensional selves. *"It will be given when you need it. . . it is in the evolvement process that you will grow and be given the answers. Understand that this is not only on Earth but on other* planets as well, and not just involving humans, but the animals. . . ."

What can we say?

The initial weekend ends with: "Bonding is the key word for you three, and aren't you lucky to have found each other!"

In between the first and second meetings, several messages come through to Joan, including the introduction of the Sirian and Pleiadian Sisters.

The content of many of the following monthly sessions includes personal issues, that, looking back now, need to be addressed before THEY can lay out what this joint mission involves. In our individual lives we need time to heal enough to be able to bond as three human beings who can be totally honest, supportive and loving toward each other — unconditionally. And we have to learn to trust, not only each other and the GROUP, but especially oneself!

We often are told to be in the world and not of it; to meditate and pray daily; to be in the struggle on Earth in order to understand the dynamics and to participate in the changes to come. . . .

At this point in the chronology, Maria leaves linear work. Joan and Maxine continue on.

During many events we are reminded that 'time' is only a factor of 3rd Dimensional reality — that these BEINGS (who we have grown to consider as our loving friends, from the 9th to the 26th Dimensions) exist in 'no-time'. During the weekend of September 12, for example, we are writing furiously for 41 pages, taking turns, our fingers cramping. We are getting some information about 4th Dimension and wondering if we will ever get a break. *"Understand we are still in this place with more information to give you, so sit still for awhile please."* We end up with 69 pages.

The Sisters from Arcturus present themselves with a message from the Goddess energies *"awakening on Earth right now in your vibratory spaces. . . .Your planet is in the process of moving into Ascension and we need to be on Earth to offer our gifts so we can become unto a higher level of being."*

We begin to "hear" the first inkling of what is to come — an especially exciting and noteworthy event for Maria, the long-time animal and Nature loving triadic component: *"It is through us that Nature is accessible to you, in that you can offer to it the very essence of beingness through asking us to be a part of you in this work. Understand that it is through Nature that you can evolve yourselves, by virtue of the fact that it has much to offer you in its abilities to help you move through emotions and to evolve unto your-*

selves. . . . *As you commune with Nature, you commune with the Goddess. . . .*"

Angelic presences make themselves known.

The November, 1997, weekend proves another turning point by virtue of more hints as to what is being asked. *"The 'threesome' is God's source of finding each other on Earth. The triad works because it stretches the mind and heart of each person to offer ideas and thoughts to each other, to expand consciousness on Earth regarding God's plan for evolvement of Earth."*

And: *"The truth is that individually, in this work, you are fearing what is asked of you. Validate that it is in your work as a triad that you can open up to these fears. Struggle to open up as individuals, but know that, as a group, you will make it happen."* Little do we understand the magnitude of these words!!!

And really getting down to the essence: *"God is rotating toward Earth to seek the help of the animals in moving Earth to its next level of Ascension."*

Ah ha!

Ever (yes, admittedly) part of physical reality, we periodically ask about various physical imbalances/ symptoms and get a confirmation that a combination of cell/DNA changes as well as glandular changes account for most of our problems, with this addendum: *"Validate there are no diseases in any of you except the disease of infectious enthusiasm. Validate we are funny. Finding you three was easy!"*

On a slightly more serious note, we are sometimes gently, sometimes not so gently, reminded of personal issues we are slow to deal with — doing the inner work required to bring ourselves into balance mentally, physically, emotionally and spiritually. Ongoing work! Among the three of us, we experience many modalities, including meditation; hypnotherapy; psychotherapy; chiropractic; soul retrieval and other shamanic healing; Thought Field Therapy; Eye Movement Desensitization and Reprogramming; energy work such as Reiki and Therapeutic Touch; use of stones and crystals; flower essences; dream study; use of magnets; medical intuitives; Feldenkrais; Integrative Manual Therapy and even some inter-planetary laser work, courtesy of the Sirian Sisters.

As a triad, we grow to understand the need to support each other and subsequently spend hours doing healing work on each other, gradually learning to be more open and honest.

Coincidence? In our December 1997 weekend, CHRIST CONSCIOUSNESS OF THE SECOND COMING enters our midst. This is a tough one to believe. But something tangible and physical happens in the room which we all experience; we ask what it means and are told that *"in that moment the Christ Consciousness became an event . . . significant in that Earth will makeover into a new paradise of Godliness, and as you embrace this concept you can move into your inner workplaces and bring this consciousness with you."* Never let it be said that at least one of us does not question whatever we receive. Is this plan firm or fluid? *"This rotation into God is made firm by its reality in the highest places."*

It is at this 12/97 weekend that the first mention of a book is revealed, not coincidentally in the context of discussing animals on a higher plane. THEY make it clear that our role is *"to open up to this level of animal communication through . . . knowingness and intuition in order to receive messages from a higher source, to offer them to the broader public in book form so they can understand these messages in a higher way."*

We have no idea that we have just been issued our mission papers! To seal the deal, so to speak: *"As you take yourselves into this world of the animals, you will make over their existence into a higher place by what you can offer them as support for their mission . . . so they can operate at a greater level of acceptance of chaos and confusion.*

These messages which will come from on high will makeover the animal consciousness to seek love in place of fear.

"This is not 'mission impossible'. However, rotating into spaces within will makeover the Animal Kingdom so Earth can host both humanity and animals in a state of peace, harmony and mutual respect.

"It is rotating inward to God which is love on high for all manner of species on Earth now — and know that everything has a consciousness, whether animal, vegetable or mineral. The initial openings to God are not only placing God on Earth in a higher state, but also within each species so that they will be able to remain on Earth and not leave for another plane or place."

We can only stare at each other, wondering what THEY are talking about.

In January, 1998, YEOMEN announce that along with other teachers and guides, they have now reached a total number of 650. We joke about that many 'beings' crowding into our little room. (Little do we know that the numbers will soon expand to 1500 and finally to 100,000 . . . and YEOMEN are later known as TRIADIC EVENT CONSCIOUSNESS.) Perhaps the joking covers up our overwhelming feelings about the invitation, the challenge to take this on. It is so hard to trust what is not tangible! We continue to get the message to do our own inner work so that we can be ready to move into a new arena.

"The answers to the questions within which you seek are also within the Animal Kingdom, and will be revealed at the appropriate time as you seek love within and without. . . .

"Place your spiritual belief system in this reality that the animals are knowing all things at this time. They cannot teach you anything unless you will open up to their struggle to find another reality on high . . . as you rotate inward each day and ask for this empowerment to support animals in their evolvement, you will makeover their struggle into a place of higher beingness with God."

That would be enough, but they are not finished by any means. *"Going into the reality of the animals will bring you to another space of Godliness on Earth, and will keep this work in a new light within each of you, in that your reality when you enter this space will not only elevate your soul level of consciousness, but will take you to another plane of existence."* Uh oh.

By February, 1998, we probably (on some level) figure the book idea has faded away since we hear no more specifics about it. We figure wrong. *"Understand, it will be your mission, should you choose to accept it, to write the*

animals' book — about their states of elevated conscious-
ness and states of stuck consciousness, because they are
Earthbound and finding love on high to be their salvation on
Earth. . . ."

When we are informed that *"the March agenda will take
you to another dimension where the animals are waiting for
you, and where you will makeover into new beings of
consciousness by waking up to who you are on other
planes,"* it of course sounds very exciting, though we have
no frame of reference for any of this except for reading
about it from other peoples' experiences. It is also during
this February session that we first hear the phrase "all things
great and small," within the context of what is to come.

We ask if the book comes with a title. *"The book allows
the title to remain unnamed until the writing has occurred,
and then you will know what the title is. Book writing is on
the March agenda and we would suggest each of you
collect ideas for its content, as you have 'knowings' in daily
consciousness. The book loves its reality and its reality
within each of you as it already exists."* This is too much.
Just to be sure we really get this right, we need to check in
again. Yes, the book is already written somewhere out
there. We just need to tap into it. This is too, too much.

Then we are blown away in the March 'event'. *"What
Earth needs now is to evolve on many levels to new spaces,*

and the book channeled to you will offer Earthlings this rotation into new ways to validate the animal spirit on high. . . . God is with you for the duration of the weekend, and offers you the grace to do this work on this plane."

And: "The animals are placing Godliness on Earth through their secret spaces this weekend, and that is the momentous event which we have taken into the Earth for all of the Animal Kingdom to behold."

Where and when do we begin to change as individuals? It doesn't matter. At one point or another all three of us realize, individually, that our lives are now about something different than what they had been prior to our meeting together.

It must have been subtle and cumulative because no one expresses a sudden 'transformation' or epiphany. 'It' manifests through a process as a more peaceful state of being. Not perfect by any means. No. But different, and better.

The inner work preparing us to write the book has begun to focus and expand outward, taking the form of visiting places where animals are more or less held captive — hatcheries, zoos, preserves — and making eye contact as part of our instruction for healing of "their inner souls which are seeking love . . . this technique will makeover the healing of animals into a higher state of reality than has been done on Earth up until now."

Another tall order, but one filled with much love and satisfaction each time we do it. Also we are filled with an expanding sense of the truth of this work.

During the April weekend a lot of material comes through to be integrated into the book. However, we still have no clue as to where to begin, what format to use. . . .

We hesitate to ask, but do so anyway: by when is this not-yet-but-actually-already-written-out-there manuscript to be published? "We suggest that the actual publication take place within the end of this year (1998). Validate that the December timeframe is appropriate for its dissemination to Earth, but the final date is still open depending on your work pace and abilities to place this on the top burner. . . . the book should be a top priority from our perspective. . . . The book leaps into publication as soon as you are able to receive the concepts which have already been ordained on high planes of existence." We had to ask, didn't we?

Each of us, at times, questions this whole process: is it real? It feels so surreal! Are we dreaming some crazy group dream? Does it make sense? Why are they asking _me_ to do this or that? The thought even crosses our collective minds that this is some kind of cruel joke! Not just the book, but all this personal stuff.

In April THEY do mention that *"The places where you will find answers for the book are found in your daily meditative work, dream state and seeking love on Earth in all ways."*

By the June weekend we manage to have a first draft, and the North Star Sisters manifest to offer their help by *"rotating into the book on all levels of preparedness for the understanding needed by the triadic components to be able to write the book in the highest way possible."*

Thank God! And the North Star Sisterhood.

By the end of June, Joan leaves linear work and Maxine reduces her work week to three days.

We discuss the whole idea of books and all the trees sacrificed for their production; we agree at the very least to push for recycled paper. The BEINGS of course 'hear' us: *". . . by what you say about trees in your book, the world will know their value and that will enable the healing process to occur."*

Book drafts covered with red pen corrections, deletions, additions travel back and forth via the postal service over the next several months. By now the work exists not only as "work," but a true passion.

In a September dyad (yes, we also meet periodically in twos) we get: *"The book itself is opening up to ways to quest after Godliness on high within the format of life on Earth for the human-animal connections, and this teaching is the forefront and the theme which should run throughout its essence and spine. As the animals have offered you their realities on Earth, and are presented within the book, their seekings have waited for the spiritual growth process to place validation on the realities within the book itself. That is why it is a work in progress, up until even its actual publication, because these truths are flowing within and without its essence such that its essence will be understood by what it manifests during its writing and reading."* WOW!

At November's meeting, we take turns reading the latest draft aloud and then after more (many more) red pen corrections, mail travel and a couple of dyad meetings to work on it, the three of us watch what we think is the final draft come to life on Joan's computer. Drum roll, please!!!

Looking back, it is interesting to reflect on how 'channeled' information flows to us through very different modes: through deep meditative journeys; through automatic writing; through use of the computer; the use of the pendulum; through flashes of knowing that simply come to mind at non-specific moments, through telepathy with animal consciousness, and through the dream state.

As the months go by, we discover too that some form of telepathy is at work among us, as evidenced from the manuscript's traveling back and forth with changes, notations, questions — inevitably one person has come up with exactly the same conclusions as the other.

In the course of pulling all this material together, we plead our case more than once about the "higher language" used by the GROUP; that is, our linear selves question how anyone will really resonate to it, or even take the time to read it! Our answer — well, let THEM explain:

"Validate that the Language of the Soul is the language known by your higher selves — but within the evolvement of humanity it is also the language which has been lost — and which is known as the Original Language.

"As the Language of Origin of ALL THINGS GREAT AND SMALL emanates forth into Earthscape, the emanation itself will raise the very consciousness of the receivers of its elegance and grace and its seeking of a higher form of Spirituality, within and without. Language of the Soul comes through these understandings, that the pureness of Soul Essence on high emanates into Earthscape within original language which is not a language — but form itself.

Validate that the essence of this emanation is pure Spirit which also opens up your essence to higher realities and higher realizations as the ALL THINGS GREAT AND SMALL concept becomes unto itself within the bookscape."

The year 1998 comes to a close and the book is, we are thinking, ready to be published. The rude awakening is that we have somehow forgotten one small fact: not many first-time authors have publishers beating down their doors.

Letters go out, phone calls are made. Nothing happens. Publishers do not respond. The Events continue through the winter and spring of 1999 and we continue to work on our own personal issues. The BEINGS tell us over and over that in 3rd dimension, free will is so honored and the planet is in such transition that the book needs to be on hold until the perfect time. . . . We wait impatiently. We do not mask our collective disappointment very well. THEY encourage us to keep the faith, to trust.

On August 11, 1999, there is a solar eclipse and planetary re-alignment such as has not been seen since the time of Christ on Earth. We get together for our triadic happening and it becomes clear that the perfect time has arrived for the book to emerge. There are no bells and whistles, no champagne, no loud cries of glee. But we know!

At some points along this journey, we have heard: "Go out into the world and do this dance with others as you teach others to seek God along the way." We are humbled by what is occurring in our lives, and grateful for the opportunity to serve in this way. It is our hope that the messages of this book convey even <u>half</u> the joy we feel in relaying it to you. Above all, we trust the Nature Kingdom will be filled with joy at the result.

Maria Grant
Joan Haywood Heleine
Maxine Hollinger
August 12, 1999

ONE
SPIRALLING
DANCE

Strange. . . . I feel as though . . . I've been here 'before.' I don't know why . . . but . . . umhmm. Yes. I'm sure I have. How magical, how heart-throbbingly, overwhelmingly glorious, how . . . almost unbelievable! *The Garden,** I mean.

Oh, I see you're smiling. Perhaps thinking, 'Ah, I get it, a fairy tale.' Umhmm. I understand. I'd probably be incredulous, too, but here I am. My 3rd Dimensional,* Earthbound imagination — rather an extensive one I might add — could never have come close to conjuring up this . . . this state of being!

Just let me get my bearings. I'm new at this. The truth is, I just got here — full time I mean. I had glimpses, but this — As I'm looking around I have a weird sensation. Could it be? You won't believe it, but suddenly I . . . I see and understand everything. At least the haze is clearing and I'm starting to — as if a blindfold is falling from my eyes, cotton

1

coming out of my ears, gloves being pulled from my hands, a bitter taste leaving my mouth, and even nose plugs off my nose! All sense heightened — tenfold. I feel so much lighter!

You may be muttering to yourself, "Who would want to be somewhere, even *The Garden*, without family or friends, or someone you like even a little?" I forgot to mention that several family members and a number of friends <u>are</u> here, not counting thousands of others — angels, guides, people and animals I know who have died over the 'years', twin flames,* some called The Sisterhood* from many star systems, and something known as Harstal* Crystalline Structures. Granted, I have merely gotten wee glimpses of them thus far.

I cannot begin to say how magnificent this is! I decided to be alone for a short while to, as I said, get my bearings. The ones who arrived with me are busy exploring *ALL THERE IS*,* which I must say is a vastness beyond words. So I will join them in exploration but, you see, I always had the desire to view the whole picture, from 'beginning' to . . . well, returning. After all, there <u>is</u> no 'end.'

I figured perhaps I could find out if — Whoa! Just now, because I <u>thought</u> it, a gigantic flashback is moving in front of me, taking me to the 'beginning' of *Creation*,* *spiralling** through galaxies, now through Earth's solar system, linear history of Earth 'time', and, finally, the amazing *shifts* that brought me here — back to *THE CENTER** of it all. Incredibly, this has happened in a flash of light, even before the thought of it was completed in my mind!

Wow!

Let me *think this* into a slow motion instant replay, in case you'd like to join me on this journey. I'd like to run through it again myself because I can't quite get a grip on all of it. It seems too fantastic. I'm really not making this up . . . It just flashed by, and I knew what was going on.

Okay, let me think it in <u>linear</u> 'time', though I must tell you it's true: there is no 'past', 'future', here, there, up, down, good, bad — not in this place. Yes, yes, I see the smile again; I really do understand. I can hardly fathom it myself and I'm looking at it!! No matter. Sit back and relax. You may feel exactly the way you do now when we've finished. On the other hand, you may not.

---

* See Glossary beginning on page 179 for further explanation of all asterisked words.

TRUE BEGINNINGS

I see seemingly endless space. A void? Oh, but now I see it is pure *SPIRIT*, pure *CONSCIOUSNESS*,* pure *LOVE*,* with infinite creative energy.* There really is no 'beginning' as such!

One of billions (or trillions?) of planets — one of the energies to emerge from *GOD'S WORD* — is Earth. The energies come from what I am seeing as outer worlds where *SPIRIT* finds sources of expansion, coming into emanation by *THE HAND OF ALL THAT IS* — energy vibrating at different rates of speed that produce the material of the Universe. *GOD* is having a wonderful 'time' with this!

And the Universe is infinite, the effect of infinite *GOODNESS* and *DIVINE POWER*. A hundred billion galaxies with maybe a hundred billion stars within, and perhaps ten billion trillion planets!!

No matter how much this infinity is broken down into star systems, planets, galaxies and so forth, I realize *THE CREATIVE FORCE* of them ALL is contained within each, like a hologram.* Now I understand the true symbolic beauty of holography!

I zoom into formation of this planet, Earth, coming from cells of *THE HAND OF GOD/GODDESS*, as *SOURCE* emanates out and into the world within its truth and seeking. As *GOD* gives life to Earth, *Creation* Process itself expands outward and inward within all keeping of *GODLINESS*. The words to express this magnificent scene just flow out to <u>you</u> from an unknown place within <u>me</u>.

Just imagine pure *SPIRIT*. *SPIRIT* energizes *Creation*, and forms take on matter and become their own *Creation* Process. As *Creation* realizes itself, *GOD* gives it free will* and therein 'begins' the story of soul's *spiralling* from higher grace into seeking of Earthliness and its densities. So 'begins' the seeming paradox of 'new' consciousness issuing from *CENTER*. Yes, we are in the image and likeness of *GOD* — <u>all</u> <u>living</u> <u>things</u> — in *SPIRIT*.

I watch this unfold in front of me and it is mind-boggling. Maybe this is a dream and I'll wake up and be as confused as ever. Well, perhaps not so much confused as *in the dark*. . . . Yet here is this reality. I seem to be very much <u>awake</u>. I see that there are other worlds with no physical bodily existence, composed completely of an astral nature. Ah, that explains life on other planets where it appears no life could possibly exist! How ridiculous that I didn't see it 'before.' I'm humbled by the immensity.

I apologize for rambling, but this is awesome to behold. The Cosmic Plan, as I view it so far, is for souls to be part of unlimited cycles of experience, of choice, in which each soul* ultimately comes to know Creation in all its dimensions.* When a soul's free will is no longer different from SPIRIT, the cycle is completed and individual consciousness merges with ONENESS so that spiralling back and forth from SPIRIT to illusions of separateness and back becomes unnecessary — on any plane of existence.

Since The Plan includes soul's experiencing ALL Creation with the gift of free will,* GOD does nothing to interfere. No matter how the gift is used, all souls eventually return to CENTER. I could never, while in 3rd Dimension, figure this out. I mean, what about really horrid behavior?

Okay. Yes, yes . . . free will. Excuse me again for rambling.

My gosh, I am seeing that as animals and other elements seek higher truth throughout 'millennia', human condition is only seeking Earth consciousness as source of higher power. Yes, free will again. But I had no idea how nature fit into the picture.

Despite all this, I see that over the 'millennia', there are always some souls who choose to remain close to CENTER.

They appear to be holders of wisdom for other souls who move into physical density. But, <u>why</u> would we be created, surrounded by pure joy, *love*, and all knowledge, and then wish to move from that state of *ONENESS*, into denseness of physical reality on some physical planet where a sort of fog rolls in and we remember none of the overwhelming light of SPIRIT? Why? Obviously, I <u>don't</u> understand everything. I wish someone. . . .

"Oh . . . mmmy. . . . Who are you?" (A most lovely being of light appears before me.)

"Did you not <u>wish</u> my manifestation*?"

"Whoa! Yes . . . I guess I did. It's just that I'm new at this instant response phenomenon." (Good grief.)

"I know . . . and I welcome you. I am **TEDSTRE** of *The North Star Sisterhood,** here to assist you in understanding ALL you are observing."

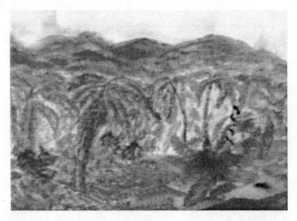

ALL THINGS GREAT AND SMALL

"From *The North Star*? Really?? Is that like Northern Exposure, or North Pole or . . . ?" (I am immediately embarrassed at my linear knowledge of astronomy, and I attempt to cover up with humor). . . . "Err, sorry."

(She smiles, putting me at ease.) "Let me offer you a short lesson . . . without a telescope! *North Star Sisterhood**
is from the constellation of northern hemispheres. We emanate from 12th Dimension,* and are here to teach humanity truths gained from Spiritual seeking over 'millennia' — within our understandings of 'beginnings' and 'endings'.

"But more about this 'later'. Let me first offer you some of Earth's history, with permission, of course. And I will answer your questions as well."

"Oh, by all means. . . . I've always loved 'beginnings' and 'endings' . . . and . . . err . . . middlings too."

"*GOD'S WORD* is really not complicated. . . . *It* simply creates consciousness of ALL THINGS on Earth. *Creation* validates higher power of *GOD/GODDESS* as it connects with *nature* itself, and also opens up pure and simple *love* along with the higher evolvement offered to your planet. . . . Are you with me so far?"

"You're kidding, of course." (I can't believe I just said that. But **TEDSTRE** simply waits calmly for the rest of my response.) "Ah . . . well . . . what exactly do you mean by connecting with *nature?*"

"Simply, all form* on Earth . . . as it seeks higher *SOURCE* ."

"And . . . higher planetary evolvement*?"

"It is seeking higher power of *GOD*, by ALL manifestation on Earth. Energies of the planet come from outer worlds where *GOD* finds sources of expansion on all levels and directs the energies into your world. As *GODDESS* energizes *Creation*, forms themselves take on matter and develop their own creation processes. And GOD gives free will to all.

"GOD offers **CHRIST CONSCIOUSNESS*** from the 'beginning,' and Animalscape* lives in peace and harmony for many thousands of 'eons.' **CHRIST CONSCIOUSNESS** simply offers gratitude to the animals at their expressions of GODLINESS."

"And what exactly is **CHRIST CONSCIOUSNESS?**"

"As offered from the 'beginning', It is simply placement of truth within the knowing of all created beings."

"It sounds so beautiful and idyllic, **TEDSTRE** . . . but I am observing what happens next: enter humanity, and everything changes!"

"Exactly so. And although expression of free will* is given from the 'beginning', Animalscape uses it to serve higher truth . Humanity chooses a very different pathway . . . and therein lies all the difference! The bigger picture is diminished as energetics* on Earth play out."

"Yes, I'm beginning to get a broader view . . . but what exactly is energetics?"

"Energetics is loss of *love* as humanity denigrates its connection with Earthscape* at large. Spirituality does not unfold throughout 'time' because humanity does not embrace planetary evolvement as sought within the original *Creation Story.**"

(I see and hear these words booming across the sky:)
The original story opens up planetary truth that all manifestation on Earth is created in equal realities as they together seek SOURCE.*
(This resounds again, louder than before.)
(Sigh). . . . "And from this 'moment' in history, it seems all downhill. . . ."

"In linear, 3rd Dimensional reality, it is so. Humanity seeks its own essence within form, rather than *higher* essence."

"Which brings me to my original question. . . . Knowing the state of the human condition, I'm still mystified why soul* would choose a lifetime within Earth's density.* Why would I have made that choice for this lifetime . . . and probably lots of others? How could it possibly serve . . . well . . . any kind of evolvement ?"

"Good question! And I hope you're ready for the answer. . . . Density serves soul in its growth into higher truth. As soul seeks Earth densities, and takes consciousness within, it expands exponentially because of the polarity between these two realities. As soul expands, Spirituality can then be *transmuted** into *secret spaces** within all life forms on Earth, so the entire lifescape enlarges."

"Oops! Screech! Whoa! Hold it, please . . . *secret spaces?*" (Sounds like . . . like a children's board game!). . . . "And *transmutation?* Could you help me out here? I confess I've held a seemingly limited view of how the Universe works, how it all came to be, what GOD'S Plan is for ALL living THINGS. I mean — I believed in the Big Bang Theory, maybe even some evolution, maybe . . . I feel pretty ignorant."

"It is not ignorance, but only loss of memory. As you become more adjusted to ALL this, total remembrance will come. I am simply speeding it up a bit. Do you wish to go on?"

"Oh, absolutely. Yes. I'm just a little overwhelmed. I'll be fine." (Uh huh. Right. Just <u>a little</u> overwhelmed.)

(TEDSTRE exudes an abundance of compassion.)

"To answer your first question, *secret spaces* are universal energetic cells which open when One connects to *GOD. The CREATOR* places them within each individual to expand One's truth at a high level."

"Hmmm, I see. So, you could say that, when we're thinking, feeling and acting from a place of inner truth, we are using the *spaces* wisely?"

"Exactly! I couldn't have put it better myself."

"Thank you . . . and *transmutation* of *secret spaces?*"

"Aaah. This is a little more complex. *Transmutation* of *secret spaces* is the actual changing of inner structures or energetic cells — as the individual seeks higher purpose. Cellular structure* itself can be reprogrammed to expand into higher vibratory openings."

"Jeez, this is getting rather deep. . . . Do you mean that *love* can expand within and beyond the individual being?"

"Truly. . . . As someone seeks *love,* cellular structures expand . . . so they are available for Oneself and other seekers as well."

"Wow. . . . This gives new meaning to the words WE'RE ALL CONNECTED!"

"Exactly so. Seeking of higher truth is largely new to Earth within the last 'decade' of 20th Century, as within this 'timeframe' understandings of Creation's interconnectedness* are being grasped. 'Previously', most of humanity seeks truths within 3rd Dimensional* reality. Now the concept of global bonding* is becoming recognized."

"Interconnectedness . . . global bonding. . . . I'm afraid I need further explanation."

"With honor. You will see the direct link between these concepts. *A soul contract between animals and humans emanates from within the Interlife* period. This states that finding of higher truth is a shared bond among ALL manifestation on Earth. Animals and humans are bonded to heal together within the process of global expansion.* For planetary evolvement to occur, it must happen within ALL consciousness. Animals are here to teach these truths to all who will listen. This concept is known as ALL THINGS GREAT AND SMALL.**"

(As **TEDSTRE** references *Interlife*, I get a vague visual image in front of me, and something is also stirred deep inside:

The *Interlife* is that period of 'time' between life cycles, after One's life review,* in which a soul is honored for the 'previous' lifetime. The contracts which soul has taken on are also assessed for 'past' and 'future' lives — within greater meanings of soul growth. The *Interlife* contract between humans and animals comes directly from SOURCE. The purpose of Earthly life is planetary evolvement, and for it to occur, it must occur within ALL consciousness.

The last words echo over . . . and over.)

"What a revelation . . . what a tall order! I had no idea . . . <u>global bonding</u>, <u>healing of all consciousness</u>, <u>animals as our teachers</u>. . . . I'm feeling as though my whole Earthly education has been sorely lacking . . . not just history books !! Could we go back to origins of the planet again so I can understand *Creation* in a little more depth?? And speaking of that — call it my limited human view — but why is it you're so interested in Earth history? Are we connected somehow?"

(**TEDSTRE** continues to vibrate unlimited patience and compassion.)

"Many questions! But there is no 'time' like the present. Be prepared to expand, broaden and deepen . . . as well as, to be, well, astounded!! Let us look again at *CENTER*. . . .

"Let me begin with my own star planet, for our history is not so very different from yours, which perhaps explains our interest in your density — oops — I mean, destiny . . . under the stars." (Her eyes are twinkling.)

(As **TEDSTRE** begins narrating, I am able to see that *North Star* interest in Earth's destiny comes from *ABOVE*, in that the higher the vibratory level of the seeker, the greater the interest in serving others. After all, **TEDSTRE** <u>does</u> manifest from 12th Dimension!)

"'History' of *North Star* goes back to a similar place of density and lost truth. Through global transition into *secret spaces*, *North Star* transmutes itself into glowing reality where *SOURCE* thrives at *CENTER*. . . . The Star itself is now able to rotate* outward into the Universe and offer truth to other planets seeking cellular light and *love*."

(As **TEDSTRE** speaks, I am fairly blown away by a display of fireworks making Macy's 4th of July celebration seem like a single sparkler!)

"*North Star* is exploding with truths to offer Earthscape. *North Star Sisterhood* feels 'historical' attachment to Earth because of similar loss of planetary *yeomen** at an early age. The *Star of the North* is said to have almost lost its sparkle!

"It is only through ALL THINGS GREAT AND SMALL truths that our planet recovers its lost *spaces* — and can be *transmuted* into higher essence. Specialties of 'beginnings' and 'endings' come from our potential extinction.

"Without further ado, let me start from the 'beginning' with an expanded historical view of your planet, and you will soon see why you are in the pickle you are in. Please feel free to stop me for clarification."

(I settle in for a 'long day's night'. . . . I mean, how often does One get to simultaneously observe, hear and experience a history lesson taught in living presence — not to mention living color!)

"As THE HAND of GOD/GODDESS seeks to open up ALL Earthly *Creation*, The Fingers form each aspect of the planet — and these include ALL THINGS GREAT AND SMALL forms — animals, vegetation, minerals, rocks, water, soil, and all the elements known at large, except humanity, which, as you know, comes 'later'. As these elements are created, they wait for direction from *ABOVE* to know what they are to do on Earth — in order to validate higher truth.

"**CHRIST CONSCIOUSNESS** *is in the world from the 'beginning' as it is given from THE HAND of GOD. But It is not known until 'later' since within Animalscape's view it is not differentiated from SOURCE. For many millennia, Animalscape lives a lifestyle of higher truth through direct connection with SPIRIT. As human form* takes shape, higher truth is not sought. Thus, 'beginnings' of spiralling downward are manifested — for ALL Earthscape* to perceive and understand.*

"*As the overall picture gets clearer, One sees what a real playing out of opposites there is between humans and animals, as the disparity between these forms continues to widen and deepen on many levels.*"

"Yes. But thankfully I see hope in the 'later' panorama.*"

"It is definitely so!"

"So much to assimilate . . . forgive me, but I'm still wondering why One would choose physical reality or form on Earth. . . . It seems we make a mess of THINGS right from the start."

"Do not think badly of human life. ALL is part of experiencing *Creation!* The answer to why One chooses physical reality is the difference between seeking *love* within confinement of form on Earth — and seeking *love* within SOURCE — where ALL is ONE. Those of us who remain close to CENTER as guides and helpers honor you who are courageous in being birthed into illusion* of separateness: searching inward to remember the light; falling into sorrow, despair, fear; playing out your roles in the illusion; doing the best you can to remember — and then evolving into who and what you truly are — pure light and *love!* It is a most difficult challenge, because when soul develops a brain and other organs, as you will see, it is capable of obtaining knowledge. This, then, explains structural changes which open up soul to free will — and to manifestation away from ALL THAT IS. . . ."

"That helps a lot. Thank you. **TEDSTRE**, how would you describe your manifestation at this point in 'time'?"

"*Star Sisterhoods** — like myself — are close to GODHEAD in our realities. Although we are in form, it is light being seeking evolvement of ALL *Creation* through ONENESS. Forms that remain light or pure consciousness continue to direct all their energies to and from *SOURCE.* However, the one thing that crosses back and forth between dimensions, *spiralling* forces of tremendous power, is *love,* which is the energetic propulsion of *unity* into ALL THINGS within sight of *SPIRIT. . . ."*

"I assume we're talking about <u>unconditional</u> *love?"*

"What spirals within outer realities is the highest form of love. Because duality is already set in motion, *love* on 3rd Dimension <u>is</u> conditional — in that a set of 'consequences' for behavior exists everywhere . . . as you will see in Earth's panorama before you."

"Yes, I see what you mean and. . . . Look! What's going on here? It seems GOD is creating a sort of soul tree and these other forms are springing from the roots . . . each form divides and becomes another — ah! —is this like a hologram? Because each is exactly like the other in intensity of light."

"The holographic concept is a good analogy. Indeed, these are souls going deeper into matter or density, yet not totally into physical form as you have known it. Neither are they yet male or female, but both. At this 'point' where they are not yet absolutely connected to the material or physical environment, do you notice anything else remarkable?"

"Oh! How incredible! Animals, vegetation, stones, water, air, soil — ALL of <u>them</u> are in astral form as well! I see it now!"

(The Sister from The North Star is smiling serenely. Suddenly, ALL is sound and vibration. I am floating . . . a part of them . . . merging with wind, trees, animals. I see why this feels so familiar: it is the sense of ONENESS. I am truly awed.)

"How do I know this isn't a dream, that I'll wake up into my physical, dense body . . . and all the chaos of 3rd Dimension will surround me?"

"But *you have awakened*.* Such is the point."

"Oh. Thank goodness! I needed that reassurance. Let's continue this . . . this lifescape. I want to feel and experience ALL of it!"

"You are highly validated. ALL in your observation is seen and heard. Wind, water, animals, vegetation, soil, stone — ALL have a language."

"I hear it now! I do! As if sound or language penetrates my cells. Is this how the pyramids or structures on other planets are built? Not by physical sound, but sound that affects atoms and molecules?" (I have no clue what provoked that question.)

"It is such. The sound used to build the pyramids, however, comes from another dimension . . . where music is the force and language of ALL higher *Creation*. . . . You are learning exponentially by the 'minute'!"

"Now I understand why certain music even on 3rd Dimension was so powerful. It penetrated the physical barrier of the body and affected my being. What I'm hearing now fills me with extraordinary . . . *love*. I'd like to remain wherever this is forever, but I also wish to experience the whole . . . *spiral*. Can I return here?"

"You <u>are</u> here, whenever you wish it."

"Oh my gosh! That's true! I keep forgetting. Well, then, onward! I see 'time' moving 'forward.' Oh — that's odd. Everything seems, well . . . disconnected?"

"Human density is increasing as each individual's soul essence* is seeking only its own source for truth . . . and there is less connectedness between beings. Although Spiritual connection is maintained, humanity's growing detachment keeps Earthscape from sustaining its higher truths.

"Interconnectedness of ALL THINGS is now lost within these early scenes and Earthscape becomes what humanity seeks: to express reality within matter."

"I observe that the ecosystem is already out of whack — even at this early stage of human development."

"Exponential losses of 20th Century species are begun even at this point in 'time', because of humanity's lack of interconnectedness with ALL THINGS GREAT AND SMALL."

"Yes, I see that now. And human evolution toward self-containment continues. As physicality is evolving, I see organs developing that are able to create heat necessary for life. As bodily fluids become warm blood, need for circulation becomes self-contained, and each individual seeks only his or her own circulatory process. Amazing! As beings become more independent, <u>external</u> objects begin to have significance, some for physical well-being, some simply objects of desire. The soul/bodies are becoming more tied to Earthly existence.

"I notice the sun is withdrawing some of its intensity, and a moon is forming from openings to another higher planetary existence. Whoa! As the sense of sight is developing, light and darkness become more differentiated, and soul's power to create itself in the image of GOD is further diminished." (I am floored by my ability to make any sense of all this. Unfortunately, it comes in spurts.)

"You are perceiving with great accuracy. And you are seeing that as soul evolves into physicality, it is seeking less and less the light, and more and more the forms of darkness."

"Good grief! Am I imagining this? Look at these soul/bodies experimenting with all kinds of *combinations* of physicality, creating experiences in physical form. There's a . . . cyclops! And a centaur . . . mermaids, minotaurs. . . . So much for fables and mythology as <u>not being real</u>!"

"Just so. And these forms are multi-souls seeking to explore life other than purely human — to realize higher truth than human condition allows, to provide for expansion of soul essence. . . ."

"Ah ha! I see how this expansion allows for greater dimensionality.* Now I understand why in these early 'ages' animals seem to possess a Spiritual life richer than humans . . . these animal beings know secrets of life, of all *nature*, I sense. In aspiring to truth, it's clear why shamans* choose animal Spirit Guides* to share the <u>secret language</u>* and fuller life of animals!

"So much to understand and rethink, **TEDSTRE**; it appears much of what I've been taught is . . . illusion and distortion. It's hard to let go of limited beliefs, and understand that perfection doesn't exist within the human condition that I am seeing. How . . . disappointing.

"Oh, my word! What the . . . is that . . . splendid creature a . . . a unicorn?!!"

ELEVATION TO ANIMALS ON HIGH

"She is. And I will let her speak for herself . . . as she comes as both *harbinger* and *illuminator* . . . of the bigger picture. . . ."

"I am **LILLIRST**, of the unicorns, here to tell you that I understand the illusion of Earthscape. I come to offer you a message of hope and *love*. We unicorns remember Earth in a 'time' before loss of *love*, a 'time' when Spirituality is truth in ALL THINGS . . . before humans arrive, the 'time' just before you are currently viewing.

"After the coming of humanity, we wait to find greater truth on Earth, but then discover that humanity does not seek greater good. We make the decision to leave in one manifestation in order to ascend before we are annihilated. We now exist in a better place . . . on 16ᵗʰ Dimension."

"I am so honored to meet you, **LILLIRST**. On Earth, I only saw pictures of you in fairy tales and on greeting cards. . . . But what happens to make you leave? What illusion do you mean?"

"The illusion is that Earth is a planet of higher truth. Animals join Earthscape with that understanding and expectation. As they seek *love* within their realites, it cannot be found.

"We are trophied by humans for display of our beauty, and realize that we are not safe in our surroundings. Understandings we bring come from other planes where animals seek higher *love* and coexist harmoniously with ALL Beings. We choose to leave Earth because our souls can become extinct, as well as our bodies . . . a concept known here as *soul loss*.*"

"*Soul loss??* What do you mean <u>souls</u> becoming extinct??"

"The extinction of a species on Earth is not contained within Earthly realities. It expands into the universe and takes away from the greater meaning of Soul itself. Soul loss becomes a loss to ALL THINGS GREAT AND SMALL and to the greater body of truth which exists at soul level.

"We do not wish to return to the planet as it exists . . . because of our experiences of annihilation and humiliation.

"Vibration* on Earth is determined by the intention of the being. Our intention comes from the highest spaces known within *Nature* Kingdom,* because of our willingness to experiment with soul essence in form. Therefore the risk to form is again put to the test, with our potential extinction. And as beings of high vibration leave Earthscape, form is diminished for all beingness. This is known as the *soul law of diminishing returns.**

"Even as we exist on 16th Dimension, our intention is to return at the 'time' of Earth's expansion. We wait for soul essence to place us once more where we are able to manifest ourselves . . . where Earth can receive our higher truths, such that coexistence* between ALL consciousness is harmonious. . . ."

"You mean . . . after all you've been through . . . you'd come back?"

"We join humanity again — as you continue to look very closely at the scenes before you —"

(She is gone — with a nod of her beautiful head.)
"**TEDSTRE**, what a gorgeous animal. Is she *real?*"

"Do you not sense her reality?"

"I . . . do, but this is so fantastic, so . . . I want to go on, I really do."

"ALL will make perfect sense as you continue to adjust to the new vibratory level — as you let go of old beliefs, and embrace the totality."

"Okay. I think I'm ready now."

"Good, because we have another visionary.*"

"Yes? Uh . . . oh, who might *you* be?" (It appears I have no frame of reference for this being.)

"This is **REDSON**, from the scape of the fairies."

(I look at **REDSON** incredulously.) "You mean you actually <u>exist</u>? It's not a fairy tale?" (Good grief, first a unicorn, now a fairy. This can't be happening. Listen, go ahead and call the people in white coats . . . but I'm telling you, this is right here in front of me. . . . Okay, I'm composing myself.)

"On 3rd Dimension, I never saw pictures that would make me recognize such a marvel! I offer my apologies.

And I'm happy to meet you! When do you first show yourselves on Earth . . . if, in fact you do?"

"The manifestation of fairies happens on Earthscape in the 'time' you are now witnessing, before the appearance of humanity. Fairies are sought after to place validation within the Treescape.* We are nowhere and everywhere . . . in that we float between dimensionalities."

"Between dimensions?? Wow!! Anyway, it's a wonder you'd want to stay on Earth once humanity arrives, the way you've been denied your real existence. By the way, where does that phrase 'fairy tale' actually come from?"

"Let me explain. The term 'fairy tale' comes from the sighting by humans of fairy essence, through the end of the animal butt (tail) consciousness. While these two realities are separate, Earthscape reality joins them together to give meaning to Fairyscape.* As such, the term denigrates both fairies and animals by placing animal consciousness at low levels. Demeaning of 'tiny things' in its midst devalues Earth, as humanity raises its own state of consciousness, now known as _ego_."

(That certainly explains a lot! Human ego getting us in trouble again!)

REDSON: "We are able to remain, through these many 'centuries', blessed with abilities to vibrate at different levels . . . and to seek sustenance through higher realities. Earth's fairy consciousness is no fairy tale in that it is sad beyond your knowing. The fairy state of consciousness is made fun of and badly misunderstood, with no knowledge of our higher seeking, our joy in living, and our ability to instill sacredness into forests and ancient trees."

"Oh, my. . . ." (I am filled with much sadness.) "Once past Earth's 'early' astral connections, with the initial 'beginnings' of materiality, so much for believing in fairies! But, how does anyone ever come up with the positive idea of fairies . . . unless someone notices you and believes you exist?"

"As you see, in ancient Ireland —Eire — and other places on the European continent, we are sighted. Ireland manifests this truth for some 'time' . . . but certainly not in what you call modern 'times.' Celtic reality of olde seeks high spaces through art, music and its rituals, but Celtic traditions eventually become diluted."

TEDSTRE: "It is only humanity which teaches disregard for the magical side of Creation. As higher truth 'later' evolves, magical 'moments' take on greater overall meaning. As Earth moves into 'time' immemorial you will see that 'moments' of magic* are the way to cross over between linear 'time' and the elevated consciousness outside of 'time.' *Spaces* where this play takes place are found in music, the singing of birds — and in manifestations where *love* radiates outward to all beings."

"Oh, my. . . . That's very beautiful. And where do you fit into ALL this, **REDSON?**"

"Our true purpose is to bring joy and life to the trees, through our abilities to float between dimensions and to offer to trees a whispy wandering within our essence — to help trees remember their higher truths. It is thus that Earth can elevate itself again through the trees' seeking. We manifest as beings of great light and *love:* As above, so below.* We take our realities to the stars, and share these higher connections with Earth."

"I had no idea." (Believe me , I hear the snickering and see the heads shaking. Either I have totally lost my mind — though just where a mind would go, I often wonder — or this is a reality beyond your wildest imaginings. Wait until I ask the next question — before you run off screaming with laughter.)

"Okay, so now that I know what a fairy really looks like, and I believe what I see . . . what about those other forms?" (Out of a corner of my seeing, I notice **TEDSTRE**'s patient smile.)

"The mermaids and such?"

"Precisely."

REDSON: "They are, in fact, Gods of Old — according to legend — who inhabit this early 'age,' before humanity comes into the picture. It is a 'time' when ALL THINGS elevate to Heaven within consciousness. These Gods manifest in all forms known, and even combine different beings into One. What is later told as mere figment of imagination is, in fact, reality, as you see it here."

"Wow! All I can say is wow!"

"I leave you now and thank you for your validation."

"I thank you, **REDSON**." (She/he is gone in a flash.)

"**TEDSTRE**, I appreciate these experiences, and apologize for any insensitivity. . . . I had no idea. . . ."

"You have asked to witness 'history' as it truly is. So be it. And speaking of connections, wait 'til you experience the next One. . . . As we leap 'forward' to 20th Century's 'end-time'.*"

(As she speaks these words, I am greeted with sensations of great splashing and playing, as well as sounds and smells of oceanic depths. . . .)

"I am **RUTSKIER**, bringing you greetings from Dolphinscape.*"

(I must confess to a slight feeling of relief at this point. . . . At least the wonderful being before me brings *instant recognition*, not to mention feelings of endearment and *love*.)

"Well, hello. I'm really very happy to meet you."

"Dolphinscape is here to offer truths within higher animal realities — as they support birthing of greater consciousness within 20th Century 'end time.'

"Dolphins *rotate* into inner worlds where our genetics store Animalscape Records at large. Earth can evolve at this 'time' only if there is a rebirthing of consciousness — available to humans simply through the asking. In order for all beingness to learn to live together, we must seek

<u>common bonding</u> to energize *creation* into elevated states. Dolphins and whales are at the forefront of these events by virtue of our shared histories and higher consciousness — sought within waters of the deep where inner worlds of GODLINESS are found and felt by ALL."

RUTSKIER finishes, then leaps higher than I ever remember a dolphin leaping, and plunges into ocean depths with a grand smile and sense of limitless joy. I am filled with both awe and excitement . . . awe for her profound magnificence and commitment to higher purpose . . . excitement because I know humanity eventually begins to see the greater picture, and what is at stake here. . . .

EVOLVING DESCENT INTO MANIFESTATION

"Oh my! **TEDSTRE**, how exciting! I see five races of humans entering Earth: black, red, yellow, brown, and white; different pigmentation to mesh with new environments of physical Earth, and varying intensity of the sun. Throughout the planet, these Spirits, in now human form, enter from ALL THINGS GREAT AND SMALL openings to GODHEAD . . . and are communicating by . . . telepathy*! This surely explains how universal Spiritual laws or principles become a part of all cultures! Realities within the planet at this 'time' are accepting of ALL life forms and are able to tolerate life in many separate variations."

"It is so."

(I am remembering a Hindu story — much like stories in so many other cultures — about the first beings in physical form. They are called <u>Swayambhuva Manu</u> or Man born of The Creator, and <u>Satarupa</u> or True Image. They have five children who intermarry with the <u>Prajapatis</u> — perfect beings able to assume material form — and from these *DIVINE* families the human race is born.)

"I now see in this story, which emanates from legends of old, that the first human beings in physical form are found within *Higher Soul Records** as 'beginning' manifestation."

"You are gaining in momentum, regarding the bigger picture. Stories from these old legends open up to original manifestation wherein humanity does not seek higher *love*, but is already validating the material aspect of formation."

"And yes, in this still early 'age', I see humanity slowly moving into its own separate consciousness, and universal conditions are affirming materiality — becoming more self serving."

"Your observations are becoming most perceptive. Do you notice other aspects of human *nature*?"

"Hmmm . . . memory is not yet totally developed, nor is language. 'Past' and 'present' are not clearly distinguished either. And 'future' is somewhat blocked. Ah! Of course. I understand. . . . That would preserve total freedom of action, while encouraging curiosity, exploring, co-creation.* Yes, I see."

"Yes! And what of the evolving laws of the physical Universe?"

"I am seeing that as a result of projecting themselves into materiality, beings are able to experience heat, cold, pleasure, pain and so on, but the more they move toward sensual gratification, the less able they are to move freely into or out of their acquired bodies. Oh! And they are now subject to cycles of birth and death, and all laws of the physical Universe."

"And what of death?"

"At this point in 'time', death surely is not considered the end — mainly because everyone sees the body as a temporary home from which to experience Earth plane. Death is seen as opening* to higher planetary evolvement. Those who die move into spaces of eternal beingness, where they can then assist those in form to move into their Spirituality. Consciousness, therefore, flows and is quite

mobile. It has nothing to do with the ending of the body. . . .
TEDSTRE, who are those wise beings I see?"

"They are the Ones possessing great power and wisdom
— teachers and healers who become ancestors of 'future'
leaders . . . but already even they do not fully understand
*how to thank the animals for their stature and grace on
Earthscape, and it is in that lacking that early humans are
already out of touch with their highest good!"*

"Yes, yes — I see it now! The continuation of the
disparity between humans and animals. . . . And form is
evolving into male and female aspects, in order to
experience further differentiation from *SPIRIT*. The now-
designated male humans are taught how to control natural
forces, to cultivate soil for growing food, to utilize Earth's
great resources in positive ways.

"What about the now-designated female humans?"

"Ah, the female manifests to offer instinctive and intuitive
gifts to planetary evolvement — and to the men — who
have taken charge by this 'time.' Women have developed
memory and thus a capacity to use experiences of the
'past,' for the 'present' and 'future.' Their hearts and souls
and a concept of good and evil come to fruition — allowing
choices. They are able to offer guidance to the male, in

order to refine and raise the meaning of his strength and willfulness."

(You notice I'm not even going to comment on *this*.)

"I see that wise beings lead in complementary ways of living in newly-developing Earth life. While soul life of women is stronger than men, with a greater ability to be in touch with what animals, vegetation, water, stone and wind communicate, even they do not seek the <u>total</u> communication possible with animals and elements."

"Your perceptions are such that I will leave you now to experience for yourself. However, if you wish clarification, ALL that is necessary is the projection of thought. And, do not be surprised if others make themselves known as you move along!"

"Do you have to leave? Never mind. I know how quickly I can manifest things here! Thank you, **TEDSTRE**, for all your help. Will I be seeing you again soon, even to just . . . hang out?"

"There is no doubt."
(She smiles that serene smile and sort of evaporates in wisps of light.)

PLANETARY MOVERS SPEAK

Okay, I'm focusing again on the early panorama —
and it's really <u>something</u>. Sound is still not formed into
words, as language, but is more the resonating with rhythms
of *nature*. As worship of sun, moon, trees and so on exists,
there appears to be a fairly close bond with ALL. Sound, as
rhythm of *nature*, validates Animalscape, but I see that it is
not wholly honored at this 'time' by humanity. Instead of
seeking *love* within the animal connection, humanity moves
toward control and subjugation — leading eventually to
human consumption of animals in every conceivable
manner.

"Excuse me. Hello."

(I look behind me, startled, and see a huge but gentle-eyed face. It is attached to a gigantic, long neck — and even more unbelievably massive trunk and legs. I am not afraid, just totally awestruck.)

"Hello yourself."

"My name is **LEARSPAN**. I suppose you can tell I'm a dinosaur."

"Uh, yes. Absolutely. I do see that you are, indeed. Wow!" (Try and find the right words to say to a dinosaur. I dare you.)

"May I further explain some of what you are observing?"

"Um. Ah. Oh, please do. Yes." (I am dumbfounded.)

"You see, animals serve as highest beings of consciousness — at the earliest 'times.' As they attempt to bond with humanity, other Earthscape realities seek to support these truths at all levels. Animals attempt to teach these truths, but are not understood by humanity. The human condition only vibrates lower and lower . . .

"We dinosaurs leave over a period of 'centuries', recognizing we are not needed on Earth. We seek refuge as the planet changes and circumstances do not permit us to stay. Earth life does not understand our purpose, and cannot sustain us within our bodily functions."

"Uh, excuse me," (I am still almost dumbfounded), "if you don't mind my asking . . . what is your true purpose, other than to, of course, colonize and energize the planet in its early 'stages'?"

"Original purpose is for us to structurally migrate into formation of birds. In such a way, we would take flight into the atmosphere and heighten the consciousness of ALL THINGS . . . as our wingedness would bring truth to *secret spaces* — and offer newness of *Creation* under *GOD.*

"Although birdscape* <u>does</u> emanate from our roots, it does not happen as originally planned . Instead, birds evolve from our remnants as our civilization is neither recognized, nor understood, for its grand purpose under the stars. Besides loss of our birthright to evolvement, Earth loses out on its original purpose as higher keeper of **CHRIST CONSCIOUSNESS.**"

(I find myself feeling both sad and fascinated. **LEARSPAN**'s animated face has me mesmerized.)

"We go to another plane where we thrive with other higher consciousness. We are in 12th Dimension reality.

"Would you like to know more — about other early species?"

"Uh, yes, definitely! I find this a bit amazing, but I want to know . . . yes! Please go on!"

"Perhaps you are not aware that during early 'times' the serpent is known as *secret* seeker of *GOD* within ALL THINGS. Coils of *GODLINESS* emanate throughout Animal Kingdom where they quest after *secret spaces* within ALL manifestation. Animals revere the serpent-like qualities, and snakes are known as Gods on Earth. It might surprise you to know that snakes On High have wings to transport and transmute them.

"Snakes offer animals higher truths. As serpents reach individual animals, the animal is then *transmuted* into a higher being of consciousness, and secrets of the Gods manifest.

"Serpents lower their expectations over the 'generations,' and as other animals take stock of these realities, they also lose their way. As serpents are again elevated to higher ways, Animal Kingdom at large can spiritually manifest. But snakes need support and connection to ALL THINGS GREAT AND SMALL. The *GODDESS*-like beings they once were take shape again, as you will see."

(I am again almost speechless with wonder). "This feels surreal, **LEARSPAN**, almost . . . as if . . . I am . . . remembering. . . . Please continue."

"Snakes are found within the psyche to perpetuate the Spiritual pathway and to evolve snakelike qualities of energy. As a matter of fact, snakes offer humanity the link with the *Garden of Eden*.* The true story is that the serpent was in *The Garden* to form a bond with humanity, but was not recognized for its higher purpose."

"Well . . . this explains use of the serpent insignia by physicians of old in those ancient 'times' when serpents are more highly regarded. So many connections are coming to me — and I'm seeing them in a new light!"

"Yessss . . . and your enlightenment will continue. So much more to tell . . . so little 'time'." (LEARSPAN gives me a large wink of an eye.) "And you think that we do not listen to your Earthly humor! Would you like me to continue now, or return 'later'?"

"Please continue." (I am still chuckling, but not to be outdone.) "I find these coils of humor most enlightening." (Sorry. I just <u>had</u> to do that. Have you ever heard a dinosaur laugh? Oh boy!)

"The Garden scene is reality within Earth Scene* on low where bonding between humans and animals is supposed to happen at the highest levels, but instead . . . you know what happens. And this is the rest of the story: the serpent role is to place validation on the human-animal bond, but the serpent's essence is rejected by the human touch and Spirituality takes a nosedive into new lows."

(Now I really <u>am</u> dumbfounded.)

"And speaking of rejection, I believe you have heard of the **Loch Ness Monster***?"

"Of course, who hasn't? . . . You're not saying that you're — ?"

"No, no. I am not." (He seems genuinely amused.) "However, the so-called **Monster** is reality only as perceived by the human eye, and only as truth is blocked through human consciousness. The **Monster** is, in fact, combined essences of many water beings joined together for protection within Earthscape, seeking higher *love* through their realities."

(Are you, the reader, still there? I understand unicorn and fairy scapes may have caused eye-rolling, but I can only imagine the reaction to a dinosaur and . . . now *this*. Um hmmm. But, stick around. There's more!

LEARSPAN's soft eyes are focused on me, as he continues. . . .)

"Finding of *GODLINESS* on your planet takes animals to where they are forced to seek *love* in strange and unusual ways. They take care of realities as best they can. . . . I believe Earthly metaphysicians call it *coping*. As animals are forced to seek *lore*** and not *love*, they are then labeled *monsters* by humanity. The irony is that humanity itself scourges Earthscape, forcing animals to seek lower realities.

"I shall end my sharing with you by saying that *GODDESS*-like animals such as unicorns and others of Earthly extinction, find their homes again on another plane — in order to manifest as the higher beings they seek to be on Earth. This place is called The Elowisian Plane,* overseen by *Sirian Sister Elowis*,* who offers animals sanctification: the opportunity to take leave from <u>Earthly</u> higher seeking."

(He makes it clear that he is finished by looking deeply into my eyes.)

"**LEARSPAN**, I am so grateful to you for this enlightenment. . . ." (I am truly moved.) "It helps me understand much more of what animals have endured."

"I am honored to serve you in this manner."
(His fantastic body shimmers into fragments of light — and is gone from my sight.)

I return to the human panorama before me as it continues to unfold. . . . Can you imagine what it feels like to come from pure *SPIRIT* and pure state of knowing, to this existence, where now memories of both 'past' pain and joy can enter the mind? Early human beings are confused by this separating of 'past,' 'present' and 'future.' They become immersed in a search for separateness and Earth's lineage.

Imagination, however, is developing. A major asset, I would think. However, the process of evolving imagination also takes humanity deeper into matter — as it seeks to own its own healing and truth, rather than connect with *SOURCE* through the <u>higher</u> power of imagination.

The most outstanding quality, though, in this historical 'timeframe' before me is the way in which early humans understand the actual environment around them. Awareness of chemical and physical properties of objects enables them to build, with no knowledge (yet), of engineering; they simply *know* weight, load-limits, space concepts — all based on imagination! They are able to lift or move great loads by mere use of their will . . . which brings to mind those great stone structures in Egypt!

Oh, but now I see that the pyramids <u>are</u>, in fact, built by other civilizations who walk Earth at this 'time' — just as **TEDSTRE** mentioned. These beings create the structures through heightened imaginative abilities because of their greater connection with truth! Sorry, humanity, you can't claim this one!

"Greetings — from *The Sirian Sister On High**** — who <u>can</u> make these higher claims!"

"No! Don't tell me . . . you're not . . . but I see that you <u>are</u>. And while on Earth I never considered myself a magician, I seem to be conjuring up a lot of amazing stuff in this place! Welcome . . . and please enlighten me further. . . ."

"It is with honor that I do so. Validate that I am **RUWNOR**, a *Sister* from *Sirian Star**** Culture manifesting into these *spaces* through your intention. I am here to validate that the way *Sirians* actually colonize Earthscape — and realize the pyramid construction — is through both thought form and sound waves. We are not only builders of

Egyptian higher structures, but of *spaces* for greater soul consciousness.

"As I open up my truth, you will experience *ONENESS* with all *Creation* offering higher imaginative abilities. In receiving this consciousness, you are able to see and remember these teachings within the acceleration process of 20th Century 'end-time.' It is with honor that I offer these truths to raise readers' vibratory levels — and to send a special salute to seekers — as *The Sirian Connection** supports Earth in this 'time' of global expansion."

(Again, as in the presence of a Great Master, I am virtually speechless. My childhood mastery of LEGO blocks somehow parades in front of me, but dissipates quickly. Still at a loss for words, I can simply say "thank you" to **RUWNOR** . . . for both her offerings and her presence.)

Still lost in broadened imagery, I hardly notice that instead of leaving my presence, **RUWNOR** seems to have expanded her essence, and is waiting patiently for me to refocus in her direction. I experience a sensation of expansiveness as I see that she appears now to be part of a *Group of Beings* . . . from *Sirius?*

"You are correct. We are indeed *The Sirian Sisterhood** with a message for you regarding the 20th Century phenomenon of *Face on Planet Mars*,* which humanity portrays on sets of stamps, and which NASA explores on a limited and somewhat skeptical basis.

"Validate that Mars is, in fact, colonized by *Sirius*. The *Sisterhood* places a remnant there to emanate forth into the Universe at large. Its purpose is to elevate the consciousness of astronomy and other galactic secrets . . . as well as to challenge and perpetuate the suspected truth: that humanity is neither alone in the Universe nor within galaxies at large!

"*Face on Mars* is formed with surface etching through a highly evolved technology wherein the surface itself is not marred. Merely through placing signals under the surface, it is perceived as visual imagery. In fact it is sonic emanation outward and inward. The *Face* represents not only the Earthly image of *Jesus*, but also the face of *All manifestation*."

(Good GOD! Are you getting all this?)

"As humanity evolves and is able to perceive at higher levels of vibration, The *Face* moves into other apparitions and forms which transmit **CHRIST**-like truths so that Earth can receive, and believe in, other life forms.

"Watch for these transmissions later in your viewing as you realize that ALL THINGS are indeed interconnected on ALL levels of manifestation."

I am dumbstruck as countless animal, human, and even insect faces float before my eyes, and suddenly realize that each is both unique and similar . . . and I'm again taken aback by the words of *The Sisters,* who have meanwhile vanished in a galactic show of shooting stars.

As I reflect on all this, the *face of a deer* appears, with eyes the size and depth of a pool, and a presence of great sadness and beauty.

"Ohhh, hello, and what a lovely being you are!"

(As I wait for her response, I feel myself getting lost in her eyes. . . .)

"I thank you. I bring a message of our plight at this 'time' and our seeking of higher *spaces.* We do not begrudge use of our bodies for meat, but are distraught over frequent hapless shootings which honor neither our beingness nor our higher souls.

"Random mutilations serve only humanity's loss of honor for all life forms. We ask that ALL humans of high consciousness speak out against these atrocities. Though a small number of humans are responsible, our numbers are indeed reduced.

"DEER also seek allegiance with dinosaurs and unicorns, who have left for a better place. We too seek a safety valve to better cope with Earthly destruction. The ALL THINGS GREAT AND SMALL Higher Connection offers us

Sister Elowis' healing plane, and it is there that many of us find refuge, as we are honored for our true essence. This message comes from higher **DEER** essence — as Voice of *ONE.*"

As this lovely creature finishes, I realize I have become almost hypnotized by her eyes, and the serenity that surrounds us both. . . . I manage to rouse myself enough to wave a sad goodbye . . . as she is enfolded by majestic trees of brilliant color. . . .

This *merging of consciousness** is the very sensation I began to experience shortly before realizing I was in this extraordinary place. Bear with me. It's difficult to translate into words. It is as if, instead of simply identifying with stone, wind, fire, soil, trees, water, animals — I (and they) *become* the consciousness of the other — merely by *thinking* it!

There is no weakening of anyone's individuality . . . not at all. In fact it creates, or opens up, extraordinary opportunities to experience Earth life. And it works both ways: vegetation, water, stone, soil, air, fire, animals — ALL are able to experience humanity. *Love* dictates all these interactions. It feels so right that I could burst with its expansiveness!

Look! A magnificent thunderstorm is approaching! Oh . . . ! I am becoming a part of it. I am strong, insistent wind, blowing wildly; I am trees and feel my leaves and

branches swaying, rollicking; I am thunder and lightning . . .
booming . . . lighting up the sky! I am cool and free!

This is remarkable!

It is *something* to merge with these other forms and
know who they ARE. Likewise, they are able to see the world
through the eyes of humans. . . .

I am so touched by all this, please give me a few
moments to enjoy the sensations.

DEEPER INTO MATTER

Magic Words

In the very earliest times
when both people and animals lived on earth,
a person could become an animal if he wanted to
and an animal could become a human being.
Sometimes they were people
and sometimes animals
and there was no difference.
All spoke the same language
That was the time when words were like magic.
The human mind had mysterious powers.
A word spoken by chance
might have strange consequences.
It would suddenly come alive
and what people wanted to happen could happen —
all you had to do was say it.
Nobody could explain this:
That's the way it was.[1]

I want to see the whole story, so the panorama moves on. I realize a basic reason for development of language, as we understand it, is that humans are beginning to lose this ability to *merge*, to look through the eyes of other parts of *nature*. I see that in *original language** all manifestation flows together from SOURCE into Earth, and is understood by all beingness. . . .

Picture the words: 'I observe this river.' If *original language* could 'speak' the equivalent would be 'As a river, I observe myself.' Or, 'Taking on my river *nature*, I go with the flow.' In this language, humanity would never say: 'The river flows through the valley,' but instead: 'The water through the valley waits to be realized within its seeking within the flow of other realities, in order to unite together to slip into Oneness with each other.' Ah. Yes. Yes. . . . I can put my hand into the river — but also my consciousness!

I see that *original language* is lost over 'centuries' because of humanity's separate consciousness, and that evolving human language comes about — in part — because humans lose their ability to connect with other Earth consciousness. Indeed, it is a poor substitute for what I am experiencing. Animals then take their consciousness within, and seek only the eternal language of the soul.

Ohhh! Will you look at the splendor of this Great Being! Front and center is the biggest whale I have ever seen. But then, One must ask how many whales have ever crossed the water in front of me??! Despite my overwhalement, I am finally able to ask:

"In whose presence do I have the pleasure of being??"

"I greet you as The Voice of all **WHALES**! You were speaking of language formation . . . and, with your permission, I offer you a great tale . . . as well as a prophecy."

"I'm all ears."

"Our story begins many 'millennia' before humanity arrives. Try to imagine a 'time' when ALL beingness precedes the use of language, and when language is not needed. Within this higher reality **WHALES** speak. These truths are within ocean waves and depths — and deep within arenas not known at large."

(As this Great One is "speaking," I am lulled into trance state by the sound and rhythm of ocean waves . . . as if buoyed up by energy surrounding me. How is he communicating with me? Rather than words, it is more like some kind of code, or signal . . . but, no matter . . . it is clarity and pureness of the message which I am understanding.)

"**WHITE WHALES*** of the deep offer humanity not only our stored records for evolving, but also signals of communication which teach ALL animals a higher network of connection. As energized through ALL THINGS GREAT AND SMALL, we can then offer Animalscape their resonation within the flow of electromagnetics.* As we heighten our essence and genetics, ALL manifestation can be synchronized together as ONE, and resonate outward and upward to *SPIRIT*.

"As this explosion of magnetics reaches upward and outward, Earth Scene* is fairly ignited with sparks and fireworks, manifesting fully for ALL to see. This scene is One you witness as your panorama moves to 'beginnings' of Earth's 21st Century.

"Animalscape rejoices at signals from the deep — as **WHALES** take front seats within this new age of expansion. **WHITE WHALES** merely ask that Earth support them through honoring realities within the ocean feast of ALL THINGS GREAT AND SMALL. They know that answers lie within fuller manifestation of **CHRIST CONSCIOUSNESS**."

(I am part of this whale and all whales everywhere, and hear *ourselves* saying all this. It is a fantastic surging of *love* and incredible power. I realize that the 'new' refers to unprecedented happenings in *Creation* — an experiment in physicality/duality. I am surrounded by clear blue-green ocean and sound . . . sound.)

"**WHITE WHALES** store Records of **CHRIST CONSCIOUSNESS** on Earth and join with the elephants who store *higher soul records* for Animalscape. But it is in the joining of ALL manifestation that Earth leaps forward and keeps its date with *GOD'S Higher Plan*, moving fully into their Original Story: *ALL THINGS are created equally and ALL THINGS GREAT AND SMALL manifest together within worship of GOD On High.*"

(The signalling stops and The Great One blithely fades into the blue of the horizon, quickly being swallowed up by illusion of surrounding sea, and for a moment I am totally lost in imagery . . . and something about **THE WHITE BROTHERHOOD.*** . . . I realize I don't know his name, nor did I thank — but then I quickly understand: human language really isn't necessary; he got my message.)

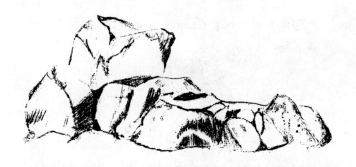

Higher Into Manifestation

Why does this loss of language occur? I can only surmise these answers: free will and expansion of physicality, and humanity's need to quest after individuality within its own species. This comes about from the earliest human lineage. Higher *love* can only be sought on an individual basis, and as greater humanity seeks its own expansion, connectedness with non-human essence slowly seeps away.

For thousands of linear 'years,' although humanity lives close to the land in a simple manner, it embraces ego structure of the mind. But here . . . ahhh . . . I see a perceptible *shift** occurring through use of crystal energy. These humans are developing remarkable technological knowledge whereby transportation in air, under water and just above ground is far more advanced than anything known in 20th Century mobility. How does a *shift* like this occur, I wonder?

"You inquired about *shifts?*"

"Uh, yes." (I am transfixed. Facing me is the most beautiful, translucent crystalline being I can imagine — shimmering protrusions of cool, quartz-like consciousness. Facets, which resonate into my presence, virtually surround me.) "Ohhhh. . . . Ahhh. . . ."

"I am **HARSTAL,*** *The Asteroid* from Lemuria,* emanating from *Lemurian* cultures of the 'future.'"

(I am taken 'aback' . . . forgetting, for a 'moment', that we are not in linear 'time'. . . .)
"Asteroid. . . . The 'future'?? There is no 'past' or 'future' here. What do you mean?"

"*Lemurian*, or MU, culture is found in realities out of linear 'time' which exist within the 'future.' Openings to *Lemuria* are available through this crystal structure, offering new ways to raise Earthly vibratory levels. As I speak, you will feel energies flow into your consciousness, as new Spirituality is evoked.

"My name, **HARSTAL**, means *reality in high things and places* — and I am from *GODHEAD* Dimensionality. My vibratory level is Infinity. I am Keeper of all Knowledge of *GOD SPACES*.

"To better understand my essence, let me offer you some knowledge of *Lemurian* Culture, which takes Spirituality above and beyond that known to exist for all 'time.'"

"Even higher than *Atlantean* Culture?" (I interject this . . . well . . . timidly, but to let this astonishing being know that I understand a little something about other civilizations. . . . I mean . . . I'm not a <u>complete dunce</u>, after all!)

"No, you are not a dunce at all. . . . And, yes, even higher than Atlantis.* A culture is only as good as the animals which partake of its secrets, and in Atlantis, the animals are not highly regarded. But Lemuria seeks to validate animals as the GODS which they are. In so doing, we find *DIVINE TRUTH* in highest form."

(Gulp . . . now that I know that my mind can be read, I'd better be sure my thoughts are . . . uh . . . pure. . . .)

"Errr, I'm sure that you know that realities of End-time*
Earth are badly in need of your wisdom, **HARSTAL**. Is that
why you've manifested here?"

"The message which I bring is regarding the *shifts*
happening at this 'time' — as one millennium ends and
another begins.

"As *shifting* occurs at deep levels, higher solutions to
living in form manifest. In embracing these changes, some
are fearful and hopeless, but Earth opens up *spaces* to be
harvested within each animal or human. . . .

"Crystal consciousness can manifest more fully through
collective use of *large crystalline structures** which take form
in Southwest United States and other sacred spaces. Within
these structures humanity can retrieve lost truths from
civilizations of old and new, high and low. Smaller crystal
structures within home settings also offer healing and *love*.

"Lemuria and other higher cultures are here to offer
wisdom to *Keepers of the Records*.* As these *Keepers*
manifest to do this higher work, their mission is now
reaching fruition within human consciousness. . . ."

"Wow! I surely missed all this in my original run-through
of the panorama! But **HARSTAL**, 'before' I got here, a lot of
my friends and I . . . well . . . anticipated some final self-

destruction of Earth because we saw all the tornadoes, floods, droughts, high winds, weather changes. . . ."

"Know that *shifting* does <u>not</u> take form in disruptive and unseemly manner, but is a gentle process through which ALL seekers of *love* move into higher realities. *Shifts* realize greater truths as technology develops and as essence itself expands. New technologies evolve from Lemuria and Atlantis, where thought processes can create higher matter.

"Use of healing crystals enables *shifts* to proceed in gentler fashion as One's inner DNA* structure is being expanded. Although higher realities emerge gradually on Earth, the process may have its bumpy spots. Gentle steering into higher truth comes from crystalline understandings that stream into the seeker's consciousness; as above, so below.*"

HARSTAL's departure is as magical as her appearance. As her elegant facets slowly disappear from my field of vision, I am aware that the atmosphere around me has subtly *shifted*. Are you as intrigued as I am by HARSTAL's message? . . . Could it be that <u>you</u> are One of those *Record Keepers*???

As I return to the panorama, I fully realize that my thoughts and experiences keep moving me into 'past' and 'fast-forward.' I apologize. But all that is happening is so exciting and wondrous I can't help myself!

At this point, this whole adventure has new meaning. I see it is no longer merely just a 'history' lesson for me. And speaking of adventures, I observe that use of crystalline structures within this 'era' which **HARSTAL** has described leads to the discovery of incredible technology. These structures are able to evolve technology into new arenas. Oh, my gosh! I see magnets being used to heal in new ways. Wow! Earth's magnetic grid* <u>itself</u> is magnetized and receives its force from the essence of the evolving human belief system. The whole thing is interdependent as cellular restructuring* unfolds.

As the panorama continues, I am going '<u>back</u>' again in 'time' seeing that humans are able to create energy for commerce and industry simply by utilizing plants. Memory is at a highly developed state. Thoughts are actually images. No sets of rules are needed. Life is presented to children in vivid images (remind you of creative visualization?) which they remember in the 'future' for any situation they encounter. Language at this point has developed, but is held as sacred. Words are power . . . words are curative . . . words can actually advance the growth of a plant!

Slowly, over 'time,' I see humans feeling personal value, ambition, power seeking, social communal life, logical thinking, forming of so-called government. All of this is initially done with some ties to *nature*. As humanity places truth within infrastructures and governing of greater communities, higher concepts appear to be lost. But in fact they are stored within the subconscious mind* — to be unearthed in 20th Century — as planetary evolvement is again sought.

Ah, yes.

Over many, many generations, beings descend further into Earthiness, into less conscious awareness of their origins. Dreams and stories passed down through the oral tradition are what keep some original connections alive. Religion develops as part of longing for these connections. What is fascinating is that, throughout 'time,' there continue to be *wise souls* who inhabit the world, keeping *nature* connection* memories alive by example and word. However, they, too, have lost connection to ALL THINGS GREAT AND SMALL.

I can tell you now, with this whole picture before me, that you will see numbers of these *wise ones* over the next 'months' of linear 'time,' as 20th Century comes to a close. Will you know them? Evolving animal consciousness is also seeking to be seen and heard — but only manifests when humanity opens its eyes to see, and ears to hear.

It is now at a 'turning point' in Earth's continuing unfoldment. Many cultures still have a rather enlightened society, with no human or animal sacrifices; they are vegetarian, women-centered, with no violent death. There are other cultures that are carnivorous, patriarchal, and war-like. It comes as no surprise when I see GODDESS Cultures* taken over by Indo-Europeans and Indo-Aryans and subsequently wiped out — from Anatolia to Egypt, and the Near East to the Far East in India. It appears these cultures are too threatening to otherwise militaristic and carnivorous societies where humanity seeks to control and be purveyor of truth mainly within ego and psyche.

It is 'later' in linear 'time'. The male and female are psychically alienated. The ancient Mother-Goddess goes "unconscious". Male psyches, for the most part, manipulate the environment through physical aggression or force — despite subconscious knowing that ALL Creation is ONE. Separate tribes which lead to separate nations are emerging out of the alienation. It is a way to experience separateness and annihilation of SELF in such a way that The GODDESS is lost to planetary evolvement.

Speaking of evolvement, appearing in front of me in this very 'moment' is a majestic, robed Being, whose wisdom shines forth like a beacon . . . and who is carrying some kind of . . . record.

(I manage to mumble a greeting as I stare at the record which appears to have a life of its own.)

"I am **THE MESSENGER from AKASHICS of OLD and NEW**, here to let The Records speak for themselves!"

"Ahh . . . excuse me. Akashic . . . what? . . . I know it <u>sounds</u> familiar, but I can't quite place. . . ."

"*The Akashic Records** are located at the soul level and contain the essence of all history throughout civilization at large, within eternal manifestation of ALL higher truth. *The Records* include every detail about every being who has ever existed in form."

"Err . . . kind of like a higher census system?"

"You have grasped the general concept, yes. The Akashic Records also serve to seal manifestation into higher truth, in that they contain only what has been translated (occurred) as already exists within linear 'time'. However, I am here with momentous news for all to see and hear, though it first requires a little background knowledge and understanding:

"*THE ALL THINGS GREAT AND SMALL Connection with The Records is now open to ALL Earthly manifestation as they are aligned with SPIRIT. This unveiling documents and validates the Divine truth of the soul bond between animals and humans for the healing and elevation of Planet Earth. It thus takes Planet Earth, of the 'year' 1999, into uncharted territory within eternal seeking of* **CHRIST CONSCIOUSNESS.** *Emanating from SOURCE, where the Records are translated into higher truth, it is with great ceremony that these realities are offered through the bookscape.**

"Understandings of The Divine Plan* itself are encoded within The Akashics, as written by SOURCE . . . thus allowing the veil* to be lifted."

"Ohhh . . . this really sounds like the inside scoop of the 'millennium'!!!"

"Decidedly. 'Reading' is accomplished through opening of higher meditative realities as realignment of human energy centers* occurs. Through opening the pineal gland* the 'eye' to see these Records manifests, as higher energy centers can then embrace greater realities. As energy centers are realigned, Akashics of Old can become Akashics of New."

"And so, you're saying that through inner meditation, One can actually read, or view, these records? Within the mind's eye??"

"Precisely so. It is a subtle process of seeking these higher realities within the altered state of meditation or chanting. The Records encompass truths of higher dimensions.

"Emanating from GODHEAD, these truths empower Earth to move from its present position of lowliest planet into the greater scheme of higher truth. Open to DIVINE seekers, Ascension* is accomplished within the learning process itself. Know that the planet is truly ascending into the stars of 'future' and 'past,' as ALL manifestation is heightened. This ends this Message of love — from THE AKASHICS."

I find myself riveted to this spot, trying to take it all in. I cannot. So please pardon me as I take a few 'minutes' to review it, because I just know it's momentous.

THIRD DIMENSIONAL
ILLUSION OF SEPARATENESS

Although it is most difficult to return to the panorama after this heightened experience, I can now do so with some hope and enlightenment. In continuing evolvement into density, another 'turning point' arrives where soul appears to attain its greatest depth into the material, physical plane. During this 'period' in classical mythology, I see it as characterized by wickedness, selfishness and degeneracy. (Look in your dictionary if you don't believe me!) Yes, all the latter are evident. On the other side of this Earthly duality are *Keepers of the Light*,* there as guides. I now see that these wayshowers* also <u>include animals with Divine inspiration</u>!

"You called?"

(I hear this but am unable to distinguish anything specific.) "Who's there?" (Oh. I realize this beingness only appears to be far away and indistinguishable because of its tremendous size and majesty. . . .)

"Ahhh, I am **ANIMALSCAPE AT LARGE**, as my consciousness flows into your *spaces*. We are here to enlighten ALL who listen within this 'period' of so-called classical mythology. We speak with a *Voice of One* as we offer the analogy of a sheep lost from its flock — and a lost civilization within ALL *GOD's Creation*. As the sheep is lost from its flock, so the self is lost from higher truth. But animals continue *to shine the light from under their bushel baskets*. They aspire to evolve civilization into realities which eventually light the darkness of the skies, and shine out into intergalactic wonders of ALL THINGS GREAT AND SMALL."

I watch in wonder as this *Majestic Presence* disappears into the horizon as quickly as it appeared, and am again amazed at all that is unfolding.

Now I see this 'period' in the context of a huge *spiralling* motion, with individual souls living, dying, re-awakening, then choosing to enter this plane again and again — in order to stretch the limits of co-creation. I can tell you, from the perspective I have, the limits have been reached.

From where does duality of good and evil develop? Is it the result of conscious separation from CENTER? Does this lack of being at GODHEAD cause Spirit, in physical form, to be diluted, weakened, susceptible? Does possibility for evil or separateness always exist, but remain unmanifested until soul takes on physical form? Does this then open up possibilities for separateness — and therefore loss of GODLINESS?

So-called evil thoughts cannot harm a Spiritual being since Spirit cannot be destroyed. But, free will and the pairing of thought with physical form, create the possibility of doing harm to another in this reality before me — and of which I have been a part. Seeking loss of love creates in itself a state of disharmony with CREATOR, and thus these realities. . . .

Beyond this dimension I'm viewing, all is harmony. In "3rd" there appears only nonsense — a distorted and limited sense of GOD. Again, the only exception is love, which opens up and transmutes distortion into higher harmony. And so does the incomparable beauty of pristine nature, in those few places where it still exists and is able to be realized from the human perspective.

I digress, because as I am viewing all this, I wonder why, if Earth life is an illusion, do we need to evolve at all? It's just an illusion, a blip in 'time.' But if there is no 'time,' all is happening simultaneously. How can this be? And if it is, what difference does it make what we do in 3rd Dimension?"

"You have many questions."

"Whoops. . . . And who are you?"

"I am **ROPHIK**, of *Arcturian Sisterhood.**"

"*Arcturus*?? Gosh. I guess **TEDSTRE** of *The North Star* must have sent you, since here I am floating around again with, well, no unequivocal answers."

"Actually, all of us heard you . . . and I drew the short straw."

(I must look <u>shocked</u>. Perhaps because I am.)

"This is called cosmic humor."

(I'm relieved) "Oh. It seems humor must be a requirement for doing this . . . sort of thing."

"Indeed, though some of us are more outrageous than others."

(I cannot help but laugh — hard!) "This is still so unbelievable."

"Do not be concerned. ALL THINGS become clearer as you continue your observation and learning. Your questions are good ones and the best answer may be found in the concept of free will. It is a most wondrous gift, such that even GOD does not intervene. However, since 3rd Dimensional reality is illusion, no harm comes to anyone's true beingness. The whole point of evolving is that ALL THINGS ultimately *spiral* back to ONENESS. It is ALL experience in co-creation, and, yes, ALL is simultaneous!

"The overall plan is that ALL *Creation* provides the stage for experiences, but eventually vibratory level rises so that illusion and reality mesh into the beauty of a higher dimension where illusion is no longer necessary. But, there are other places within limitless *Creation* that can serve the same purpose . . . thus the *spiral* continues."

"I'm sure that everything makes sense to you, but I confess I'm still a bit confused. Maybe it's my logical mind. If we can just continue my flashback/forward? And if, no . . . not if . . . when I hit a snag, could you just jump in?"

"It is done."

"Okay. . . . I see this illusion of separateness filtering into human lives and now I understand it to be the lowest 'time' in physicality, because it denies *UNITY, ONENESS*. In essence, it denies SPIRIT. In the most global perspective, the antithesis of wholeness and interdependence is separateness, breaking down, devaluing. Fear is at the root of the latter; *love* underpins the former."

"You are keenly observing the illusionary aspect of love and fear in 3rd Dimension."

"I witness scenes of slavery, violence of all types; bigotry, prejudice, racism; civil wars, which, as I see from this perspective, appear as persistent forest fires, the flames and smoke dying down and seeming under control in one place, then look — over there — another flare-up! Sometimes many are going on at once: all are forms of ignorance and domination. This is a point in Earth 'time' which I find especially difficult to look at. From here, the view (which I requested, I know) illuminates the concept of free will taken to its lowest common denominator.

"Yet, I see that it is all illusion, like mirrors at a carnival. What is seen in distorted mirrors is an illusion of what we really look like. Despite this knowing, and the deeper knowledge of *ONENESS*, it's disconcerting that humans choose to reduce free will to such depravity. What are we doing with our brains and sensibilities?"

(**ROPHIK** quietly watches with me as I rave on, then speaks softly. . . .)

"Part of what is happening is the result of *GODDESS* energies being forgotten, pushed aside. We, of *Arcturian Sisterhood*, open up Earth for renewal of these energies. *The Sisterhood* confirms that *GODDESS* energies are alive and well as they emanate from other planets — and are here to serve during 21st Century evolvement of ALL THINGS GREAT AND SMALL.

"Continue, please, with your observations, and I will return whenever you request it."

"Thank you, **ROPHIK**." (She becomes part of the non-illusory beauty around me. I am sorry to see her leave . . . but . . . I am aware I can place an emergency call whenever needed.)

As humans further separate — mentally and emotionally — from *nature*, it's much easier to see forests or groups of trees as so many board feet of lumber; to see untouched land as something to be developed; to see wild animals as game or sources of fur, or simply pests to be eradicated. *Nature Kingdoms* are viewed as <u>different</u>, and therefore having little or no intrinsic value. I see how easy it is to exploit, oppress, ignore. How easy, too, it seems for humanity to objectify those fellow humans with whom one cannot identify or empathize; how easy to get into power games of domination and hierarchy when value is based on usefulness or profitability — or the underlying assumption of "better than."

I see humans restricting the concept of GOD to a white male. What limitations are put on the very CREATOR of all! I see "might makes right" becoming an overriding value, as does competition; and a life of ease and luxury becomes a god to worship. And speaking of worship . . . um hmm . . . in the name of religion I see wars, martyrs, killing heretics, and competition for members, money, missions and property.

As I watch this life scene globally displayed before me, I see countless examples of <u>opposites,</u> along with the idea of <u>separateness</u>. But no discussion of polarity is more basic than that of male/female, because almost all humans identify with one or the other. There are really no points along a continuum such as exist regarding religious preferences, politics, values, racial mixes and so on. . . .

Aside from the fact that a woman cannot produce sperm, and a man cannot produce an egg, there is no characteristic, quality, or capacity in the male and female that is "programmed" by GOD — emotionally, physically, mentally or spiritually. It is cultural, personal, and historical programming that produces differences, beliefs, assumptions, stereotypes. Do you find this hard to believe? From far back in 'time', cultural taboos limit the expression of male/female elements in an individualized manner.

And the same applies to differences along racial lines: there is no emotional, physical, mental or spiritual capacity programmed by *ALL THAT IS* for black, yellow, brown, red, white or multi-racial humans. It is the sum total of cultural, personal, historical programming that allows for prejudice and stereotyping beliefs . . . resulting in oppression of one group by another . . . and based primarily on fear in one form or another.

COST OF SEPARATENESS

How remarkable! A *Code of Law*, if you wish, comes into existence when humans take on physical form. The same Code is given later to Enoch, then passed on to Moses and the prophets. The Essenes* preserve it — and teach it to **JESUS**, who in turn, passes it on to his followers. The words pass before me, resplendent against the sky:

> **GOD** hath raised up witnesses to the truth in every nation and in every age, that all might know the will of the Eternal and do it, and after that, enter into the Kingdom, to be rulers and workers with the Eternal.
>
> **GOD** is Power, Love and Wisdom, and these three are One. **GOD** is Truth, Goodness and Beauty, and these three are One.

GOD is Justice, Knowledge and Purity, and these three are One. GOD is Splendour, Compassion and Holiness, and these three are One.

And these four Trinities are One in the hidden Deity, the Perfect, the Infinite, the Only.

Likewise in every man who is perfected, there are three persons, that of the son, that of the spouse, and that of the father, and these three are one.

So in every woman who is perfected are there three persons, that of the daughter, that of the bride, and that of the mother, and these three are one; and the man and the woman are one, even as GOD is One.

Thus it is with GOD the Father-Mother, in Whom is neither male nor female and in Whom is both, and each is threefold, and all are One in the hidden Unity.

Marvel not at this, for as it is above, so it is below, and as it is below so it is above, and that which is on earth is so, because it is so in Heaven.[2]

Well, now. After all I have seen, heard and felt, I believe I understand most of this code. But, I must admit there is one part I just don't get —

"Oh — no — **JESUS CHRIST!!**"

"Yes."

"Glory be. Oh gosh. I'm sorry. Excuse me. What can I say? . . ." (HE is right here in front of me. I can't believe it. Yes. I believe it. Oh Jeez. I am composing myself. HE is total patience, love, compassion — and his eyes — oh they are beyond. . . .)

"Perhaps I can help."

"Oh yes . . . good . . . thank you. What was it I didn't get? Let me think. . . ."

"I believe it is the part about 'in every man and woman who is perfected'?"

"Yes, yes — that's it! I mean . . . no . . . do you mean that for a man or woman to be in perfection they must be married and a father or mother?"
(This incredible BEING is unconditional love and warmth. I cannot . . . really, I cannot be uncomfortable any longer.)

"Translation of these verses is only literally understood in the context of the original Bible version, and in truth the meanings are not as written here. The truth is that every

woman is perfected within her essence just by being open to
THE WORD of GOD, by manifesting on Earth and seeking
her purpose and truth within form itself; and so it is for every
man perfected within the same essence that it is not
required to be a husband or father, but to only be within his
Spirituality as he seeks higher truth.

"Does this clear the picture for you?"

"Yes, it does. I thank you." (Is that a . . . yes, it is . . . a
loving smile on His face.)

"I am pleased that you see so much more now than
when we last walked together."
(HE is gone. I am overcome. . . .)

❊ ❊ ❊

It took me awhile to get back to the panorama after this
last encounter. Thank you for waiting.

I think I'm on to something now, so bear with me as I
reminisce. Earliest followers of Law, and **JESUS** himself as
Teacher of Law, eat no flesh, are pacifists, have no part of
greed, live in harmony with *nature*, and share what they
have with the poor.

According to 'historical' records, pre-Christian Jews,
known as *Essenes*, are traced back to the Maccabean Age

and even 'earlier'. They are described as a unique race, remarkable, full of virtue. The term *Essene*, in Hebrew, can mean "the pure minded," "the holy ones," "the ancient Saints or elders." It becomes clear that the word *Essene* is actually more a title — and not the name of a certain sect; therefore, any such individual could rightly be termed an *Essene*. The Dead Sea Scrolls contain a wealth of information on these Holy Ones, and some of the scrolls are yet to be translated! Are these the lineage of the *wise ones* of the early 'ages'!?

Continuing my observations, The *Essenes*, referred to at **JESUS'** initial 'time' on Earth, are skilled herbalists; have an accurate knowledge of science and astronomy; are known for their care of orphans, the aged and the ill; offer no human or animal sacrifices; cherish the creatures of GOD and show them respect; live long, basically disease-free lives, often to 120 years of age; work the soil, and live only on what it produces!

Because their lives are in such direct contrast to typical living standards of the Roman Empire, The *Essenes* — and anyone like them — are considered heretics or fanatics. And, now, as I am seeing the whole picture, I see that, yes, indeed, **JESUS** himself is an *Essene* . . . and it follows, then, why he incurs the wrath of those in power!

As the panorama moves on, I see witch hunts, government atrocities, genocides, sexual, physical and

emotional abuse . . . child labor . . . ethnic "cleansings" . . .
workplace atrocities . . . murder . . . dark ages of barbarity,
ignorance. . . . The Inquisition . . . shamans of all cultures
denigrated and forced to go into hiding. . . . Holocausts . . .
harm done to others because of their sexual orientation,
nationality, skin color or religion. I see fear hovering around
all this, an absence of *love*. So, this is what **ROPHIK**
meant. . . . *GODDESS* essence is extinguished!

Mass industrialization is now taking over and I see it
diffusing urbanization over a large portion of the world,
shifting economic production from family to a workplace
away from home. It draws large numbers of poor women
into factory work at lower wages than even exploited male
workers. Men, drawn away from farms or other home based
work, become more disconnected with home.

In the 'eons' (linear 'time'!) since humans first take
physical form, the connection between humanity and *nature*
slowly diminishes to almost nothingness. I see the same
process that creates separation between the sexes has a
ripple effect between most humans and the natural world.
Components of *nature* — animal, water, soil, vegetation,
stone, air — are now seen as "lower," subordinate, existing
for the use of humans (who of course are part of *nature*, but
seem to have forgotten it.)

For sure, within the Industrial Revolution, the polarity
takes on greater manifestation, as natural things become

objects to be possessed, dissected, categorized. The physical natural environment becomes an adversary, something to be controlled (perhaps because of its very separateness.) Twentieth Century humanity becomes captive to energy intensive systems, becomes dependent. Most on the planet lose the ability to make their own clothes, grow their own food, provide entertainment for themselves or in community groups.

I do not like what I see; I am appalled, because with heightened awareness, it is all so glaringly incredible! Thankfully, I can see the whole picture, or I would sink into an abyss of depression. As it is, I am observing and relating it to you to provide a perspective — and to lay the foundation for what happens 'afterward.'

So, what is before me? An overwhelming tangle of scenes: soil erosion . . . clearcutting of forests . . . building on flood plains . . . filling swamps . . . dumping toxic waste into oceans and other waterways . . . burning off industrial waste . . . oil spills . . . cutting down ancient trees for furniture and other goods . . . destroying rain forests . . . toxifying the air . . . inventing machines that destroy anything in their path . . . spraying toxic chemicals on vegetation and into soil . . . creating billions of tons of garbage with no way to safely dispose of all of it . . . nuclear waste. . . .

Capturing animals for zoos . . . poaching . . . boat propellers cutting manatees . . . fishing line and hooks left in water, entangling water birds and fish . . . fly swatters, fly paper . . . slaughtering elephants for ivory . . . whaling . . . porpoises caught in tuna nets . . . clubbing seals, porpoises and other sea creatures "competing" with fishermen . . . dog racing . . . horse racing . . . "veal" calves . . . shooting wolves from helicopters . . . poisoning coyotes . . . dolphins captive in aquaria . . . sport hunting with guns, bows and arrows . . . horsemeat . . . steel jaw traps . . . glue traps . . . mouse traps . . . pesticides, fungicides, insecticides, herbicides . . . getting rid of wild horses, deer, other wildlife "encroaching" on human territory or economic interests . . . controlled burning to increase "game" . . . "game" preserves . . . pigeon shoots . . . circus animals . . . roadside zoos . . . cock fighting . . . dog fighting . . . bull fighting . . . animals roped, tied, subdued in rodeos . . . cattle branding . . . "breaking" horses . . . factory farmed pigs, chickens, turkeys, cows . . . slaughterhouses . . . movie animals not protected by humane laws . . . insects, rodents, rabbits, monkeys, dogs, cats, pigs used in psychological, cosmetic, space flight, medical, drug, military research . . . putting live lobsters, crabs in boiling water . . . animals as prizes (like goldfish in tiny bowls) . . . most fairytales and fables . . . electrocuting, poisoning, clubbing animals in order to obtain their fur . . . buying and selling exotic "pets" . . . ritual animal sacrifices . . . mules carrying heroin in their stomachs . . . dissecting animals in schools . . . catching insects for display . . . unwanted, neglected, abused companion animals . . . puppy mills . . . wanton breeding of cats, dogs . . . chaining dogs outside with little or no meaningful contact with anyone . . . millions of companion animals put down in shelters yearly . . . extinction of 500,000 to 2 million plants and animals (including insects) by the year 2000 (the first recorded extinction I observe is in 80 AD — the European lion) . . . "docking" tails and ears on certain breeds of dogs . . . declawing cats . . . overworking camels, mules, horses to the point of exhaustion . . . alligator-wrestling. . . .

Degrading terms like birdbrain . . . a real pig . . . beating a dead horse . . . eating crow . . . crazy as a loon . . . snake in the grass . . . easy as skinning a cat . . . killing two birds with one stone . . . a real dog . . . eating like a hog . . . stool pigeon . . . leech . . . lone shark . . . skunked . . . you bug me . . . fly in the ointment . . . butterflies in my stomach . . . what a beak(nose) . . . waddles like a duck . . . he's squirrelly . . . son of a bitch . . . jackass . . . monkey's uncle . . . dirty dog . . . weaseling out . . . you're being chicken . . . a real black widow . . . bat out of hell . . . mule-headed . . . hounding me . . . ugly duckling . . . all over me like an octopus . . . bee in the bonnet . . . WASP . . . slow as a snail . . . a real piranha . . . sheepish . . . goosed . . . buck tooth . . . hare-brained . . . stubborn as a mule . . . fat as a cow . . . hippo . . . rat fink . . . dog breath . . . horse's ass . . . worming out of something . . . crabby . . . pig pen . . . slothful . . . bull in a china shop . . . smell like a skunk . . . clumsy as an ox . . . dog days of summer . . . bullshit . . . bats in the belfry . . . a real vulture . . . clam up . . . you're a shrimp . . . pesty as a mosquito . . . ticked off . . . goat-headed . . . horny . . . bull or bear market . . . wolf whistle . . . hen pecked . . . naked as a jaybird . . . wolf in sheep's clothing . . . don't give a hoot . . . catty . . . drunk as a skunk . . . being a guinea pig . . . mousy . . . hairy as a gorilla . . . old coot . . . albatross around my neck . . . monkey on my back . . . a real slug . . . that's horseshit. . . .

"ROPHIK, help!"

HANDICAPPING OF
COMMUNICATION

"I am with you."

"This is too much. What's underneath all this bleakness that I'm missing? Help me understand."

"All is not lost . . . many are working to help *Nature* Kingdom. There are also phrases which enhance the dignity of animals: wise as an owl, eager beaver, lucky duck, lovey dovey, foxy, sweet as a honeybee, doe-eyed. . . . And animals appreciate all the humans who connect with them and are putting forth effort.

"But to help further understand the higher picture, know that each animal who joins the human condition seeks only *love*. Many animals cannot exist unless they receive higher *love*, because humanity does not provide the *love* needed.

"Animals cannot *love* themselves in 3rd Dimension unless they receive validation from other beingness on Earth. Therefore, GODLINESS does not exist for most animals because they do not receive this validation — from each other, from Earthscape, or from humanity. ALL are virtually communication handicapped.*"

"I didn't realize . . . oh . . . now I am seeing what a basic lacking this is, since love begets self-esteem and self-esteem is basic to good communication. Without *love* of self, there <u>is</u> no self-esteem. . . . I can see where this is going, and it's not a pretty picture for Earth!!"

"Yes, and the communication handicapped are found on all levels . . . in that human condition in general is locked into desperation. Earthscape only waits for higher realities . . . but conditions continue to seek *lore,** not *love,* for animals."

"Help is definitely needed!"

"As communication opens up, animals and humans together not only <u>manifest</u> in higher ways, but also find Earthly paradise at deep soul levels."

"I see that. I do. What about "survival of the fittest" within Animal Kingdom itself? How does that fit in with what is going on?"

"The concept of 'survival of the fittest' is 3rd Dimensional at best, and violates the reality for which GOD creates animals. They <u>seek</u> to *love* each other in higher ways, but need humanity's support. Take the panther, for example, who is stuck in the reputation of aggressor and predator.

"As humanity waits for the panther to seek its prey and kill again, the panther waits for Spirituality to take on new meaning within Earthly conditions. As the saga of struggle continues, the panther knows there is more to life, but is held captive by Earthscape. It is only through the coming changes that the saga becomes an altered vision of GODLINESS.

"Animal consciousness leaves much to be desired in the present view, but necessary changes are 'later' achieved through heightened techniques and their *transmutation* into Earth. Animals wait for these events with great understanding and soul seeking. The panther stalks its prey through the waiting process, but seeks *love* only through watching and waiting for changes."

"ROPHIK, I know now how ALL this does change, but feel mired in the process as I view it; it seems so hopeless."

"It is understandable. Do you wish to move past this?"

(Sigh) "No. . . . I want to experience it fully."

"You are honored for your courage and openness, and we will go on. Animal consciousness knows it is often found within the slaughter state . . . where it is sacrificed for human consumption. This reality saddens animals, but they know it is also a planetary convention held by many. Animals only ask that they be eaten <u>in a state of gratitude</u> at this 'time'.

"But they also seek greater ways *to be* on this plane and co-exist with humanity — to enjoy their own lives without being sought as sustenance. Animals seek higher goals and dreams for ALL on Earth, such that there is a higher honoring of life in its totality."

"So, all this 'time' they continue to seek the greatest good for Earth — but wait to find higher truth? What incredible endurance and patience!!!"

"How true! Their purpose is not animal *lore*, but truth as GODDESS meant it to be on Earth. Animals seek *love* on levels where humans are not able to do so . . . in that they can manifest themselves into other realities, and are able to be in more than one place at one 'time'."

"Whoa, wait a minute! Did I miss something? Yes, obviously I did. Are you telling me that *animals can be in two different dimensions at one 'time'*?!"

"I am."

"Ay yai yai. This is really getting complicated — but definitely go on."

"Cats are developing this ability at a surprising rate as they seek Spiritual manifestation. They initially seek *love* through bonding with a human being. In this process, the cat then *transmutes* the bond into *love* on a broader scale, so that it can open up new ways to greater communication.
"You were acquainted with a number of cats in 3rd Dimension, were you not?"

"Oh, indeed. Quite the little characters, every one of them!"

"Then you undoubtedly sense *deeper meaning* in the cat's *purr*. And the higher essence of Animal Kingdom cannot be felt unless One is Spiritually open! Cats understand their limited reality within Earth's confines and offer their purr to humans to sustain the higher relationship, and to keep the person interested in cat *spaces.*

"As cats seek *love* through connection with their persons, reality is elevated to new levels of consciousness, thus offering the same higher seeking — if the person is tuned into this potentiality.

"The purr stirs up a crossover into human reality, such that dimensions blend and the person can seek *love* on all levels. True cat lovers understand this dimensional *shift,* even if unconsciously. Through rapport with their cat, they are seeking *love* on higher and deeper levels."

"So cat sense* On High is really the cat's meow!"

"And here is someone who will validate that."

(**ROPHIK** mysteriously disappears again, and in her place. . . .)
"Excuse me . . . you called?"

"Oh, hello. I didn't, no, I don't think so, but hello! . . . And you are?" (I'm looking at the most stupendous dog I've ever seen!)

"Yes, I AM."

"Excuse me?"

"I AM. YOU ARE. EVERYTHING IS. Just a little multi-dimensional humor."

(I have to giggle).

"I am **RONAR*** *the Magnificent,* GOD'S Top Dog, if you will."

"GOD'S Top — ?"

"Do you believe <u>human</u> beings are the only Ones with a direct line to *THE CREATOR of ALL?*"

"Well, I . . . . I guess I never thought about it quite that way."

"Thinking does appear to be a part of the problem for humans. Too much thinking, not enough feeling, sensing, knowing. . . ."

"After what I've been observing, I'd have to agree."

"Do not despair. What you are witnessing now is only the 'beginning' of remarkable change."

"I can see that — and remember sensing it in the last 'years' of 3rd Dimensional living. Yet, it's disheartening to see all this again. . . . Could I ask what your role is, as . . . as Top Dog?" (There you go again, snickering. Um hmmm. Let's just give this a chance, shall we?)

"Absolutely. I embrace the essence of ALL animals and 'make over' their essence — as they permit — so that their cellular structures can be realigned with higher truth . . . as *THE DIVINE PLAN* prevails within the hearts of Animal Kingdom.

"For example, as the cat seeks higher *love*, it is able to transform realities through its tracking.* Tracking is the cat's ability to focus on higher realities as they are presented and then to offer healing to its companion person. Its higher sense is received internally through telepathic messages. This technique is a form of Reiki-type* healing, where the cat sends vibratory sense into the human on an energetic level. Unique to cats at this 'time', this healing offers a confirmation of Spiritual awakening.* Cats exist in the 'moment.' Take cat sense into humanity, and you manifest life only in the NOW."

"Yes! Yes! I remember <u>now</u>." (A little 3rd Dimensional humor. . . .)

"Very well done, I must admit." (**RONAR** does seem amused — in a regal sort of way, but does not miss a beat. . . .)

"And, cats are currently able to *transmute* cellular structure at DNA level. Higher Catscape* emanates into Earth with *secret spaces* for humans receptive to these truths. Cats are more evolved than other animals at this 'time' because of their dual nature: their historic connection with humans, along with their ability to be solitary."

"I see that the cat nap* . . . is so much more than a nap!"

"Indeed. Cats demonstrate abilities to bond with humans and be *wild* as well. Surprisingly, the cat is much more connected with *the wild* than with the home, though it learns to be docile and domesticated to connect with its person. In reality, the cat spends much 'time' connecting with *the wild*, in order to keep in touch with those *secret spaces*. 'Future' healing of wild animals is directly linked to cats' abilities to be in <u>both spaces</u>. As **CHRIST CONSCIOUSNESS** aligns with ALL THINGS GREAT AND SMALL, the connection is made between cats and wild animals, and this elevates into the healing needed for higher *wild things*. *Seek the eyes of the cat — and you will learn exponentially about higher realities.*"

"This is pretty amazing to me. I'm so sorry I didn't know. . . ."

"You could not know all this at the 'time' in question. But you do now, so there is no loss. Cats understand."

"Thank you for saying that. To tell the truth, **RONAR**, I'm just getting used to the fact that in the material, relative world, linear 'time' has been made all-important. In this reality of *THE ABSOLUTE*, there is no 'time.' Everything is simultaneous. It's a concept I tried to understand while in 3rd Dimension, but I must admit I had no idea how phenomenal it really is!"

"Indeed. 'Time' is of the essence! And moving from cat sense to animals at large, they <u>are</u> able to take themselves to other planes, as **ROPHIK** has mentioned. Using higher *spaces* of their 6th Dimension consciousness, animals are able to tolerate horrendous conditions on Earth.

"Rest assured that they would not stay on Earth without benefit of 6th Dimension's safety valve. Animals who leave for healing go to another plane, where they are shown that their lives are not in vain. At this point, they are fully alerted to Earth reality, and wait for humanity to take them to higher spiritual places . . . but they do not wait forever! They leave if their species is threatened to extinction — manifesting on another plane where they wait for *GOD* to alert them to return."

"I'm so glad there is a safety valve available, but it wouldn't be necessary if humans weren't operating from a fear-based mode. Many times I grieved at seeing so many species of animals abused while on 3rd Dimension. It is still difficult to see. Compassionate people are working hard to stop these behaviors."

"I would like to say that we are encouraged and inspired by the work of animal rights people, as well as those who pray for, do healing on, or simply show kindness toward Animal Kingdom."

"Thanks for that acknowledgment, **RONAR**. . . . Could we back up a 'minute' here? When you say that animals can leave for healing, do you mean while they are still in Earthly form?"

"Precisely. Animal consciousness *rotates* its essence into 6th Dimension at will, where it receives healing and enlightenment. It then returns to Earth, knowing that it is validated at soul level."

"Absolutely amazing. . . . I am astounded by all of this. . . . Good grief! Is that a . . . a *tree* . . . speaking?"

"It is. . . . Allow me to honor you with the presence of **SAMANTHA**."

"**SAMAN** —?"

INTERCONNECTEDNESS OF ALL THINGS

"I am **SAMANTHA**, who offers *inner vision of the tree state* on Earth as you observe it now."

"I'm very happy to meet you, **SAMANTHA**. . . . It's not often I get to speak with a . . . tree."

"And I, you! It is with joy and renewed faith that I greet you. . . . Trees are an inner reality on a level which does not come through to most humans. Although *trees have it*, in terms of higher understanding, this fact is 'currently' lost at large.

"ALL manner of *higher things* come through trees. . . . Tree consciousness flows into Earth on an ongoing basis but is not seen or felt by most of humanity. The synergistic effect* of trees and other elements of consciousness offers truth which is beginning to be understood. This effect is seen in the force with which trees can withstand turmoil of high winds and other turbulence.

"Trees take cellular energy of pollution and *transmute* it into truth, then take Earth's deeper meanings and offer them at large. During this period of global expansion, trees are receiving new consciousness from *ABOVE* and sending it to the planet at cellular levels. As humanity develops higher understandings, trees begin to respond with messages of hope and truth. Trees and other vegetation rotate from *GODHEAD,* from a place beyond human linear understanding.

"*Ancient trees* take you to their realities where they forlornly seek only understanding of their mission on Earth — that they are still able to serve in some small way. These *ancient Ones* take hope from those few who continue to validate them within their Reiki*-sent messages, their hugging, or their prayers.

"These trees wait for Spirituality to be found again within the human connection they once knew. They are dying in some places from <u>lack of connection</u> to anyone or anything . . . and only seek recognition and solace for their condition."

"I'm so glad I took 'time' out on my hikes to hug trees. It makes me feel good to know what it means to them! Thank you, **SAMANTHA**."

(She of course becomes ONE with *Treescape*,* and is gone. . . . I plan to manifest her and all the others again 'later' because I have barely begun to ask all my questions. But I will do that on my own 'time'.)

RONAR: "Know that GOD/GODDESS, who sits within the circle of ALL THINGS,* brings only goodness to all who seek higher reality — and it is only within this context that animals speak to the masses.

"*It is **JESUS** who says that ALL THINGS come to those who wait for GOD, alluding to this reality when **HE** speaks of finding SPIRIT on the inside and outside* of Creation.*"

(**RONAR** fades into surrounding colors and sounds of Creation. I'm left with oh so many questions again!)

I am moved by all of this . . . by the <u>great courage</u> of Animalscape. . . .

Give me a moment to regroup. . . .

❋❋❋

Okay, I now *think* myself back to the panorama. Spirit, which is our true self, knows ALL there is to know, is capable of living in total harmony. So why has Earth life been so horrendous for so many? I am mystified. If I stub my toe (while in physical form) my whole body immediately begins a cooperative effort to heal the damage done to those particular cells. It <u>should</u> be no different on a global level. If One tree, One animal, One human is hurt in some manner, the entire body of beings suffers, including Earth itself — as a living entity. If One being sends out healing, ALL benefit: *interconnectedness* of ALL *beingness*.

Still, the *mystery.**

Aaah . . . maybe a part of uncovering the mystery is this unfolding I see: *The meaning of Sabbath, as* **JESUS***, Master of Love teaches, is one of the ancient mysteries He brings to light, though few choose to hear or believe. He lives on Earth for a relatively brief 'time,' to manifest evolution of spiralling consciousness — and to teach that Greater Sabbath* is actually completion of the Universe.*

As these understandings manifest, in the twinkling of a star, I am almost blinded by lights surrounding me. . . .

"Sisterhood On High,* within Starscape, brings this message: **JESUS** teaches that the meaning of Greater Sabbath is that the purpose of Earthly existence is understanding that Earth is ONE ENTITY which opens up to higher essence through acknowledging ONENESS OF ALL CREATION.

"Realization that every soul eventually finds Greater Sabbath is shown within **JESUS'** Ascension to GODHEAD — and within this transcendence Earth realizes its highest truth."

(I thank The Sisterhood and am left feeling the richness of their brief message — and the implication of what I know is imminent!)

Coming back to the panorama which blatantly reflects lack of interconnectedness, ONENESS, I am reminded of the fact that in a society based on truth, there is no elevation of one ethnic group, race or religion over another. ALL ARE ONE. This concept finally begins to seep into my very being.

The same negative premise which exists for sexism, racism, fanaticism, chauvinism, or any "ISM" . . . exists for speciesism.* Human concern and empathy traditionally expands outward from self, immediate family and friends, to neighborhoods, personal groupings, race, religion and nation — putting Nature Kingdom at the outermost part of the circle, thus giving substance to the general assumption that humans are entitled to certain rights which animals are not.

A line from Loren Eiseley's <u>The Unexpected Universe</u> surfaces in my mind:

"One does not meet oneself until one catches the reflection from an eye other than human."

And, as I hold this thought before me, I am reminded of the innocence and wonder of a small child before the illusion of Earthly realities . . . and now I am beholding *Essence of a Small Child!*

"**Children of Earth** at this 'time' are networking within **CHRIST CONSCIOUSNESS** and wish to make known that their essence is pure and true — as they wait for the 'moment' they are called to raise their voices as *ONE*.

"Watch for those exceptional children who reach out to adults and offer gifts of higher essence. Validate that children under age six are those most highly interconnected with each other. These children are receiving what they need to heal — and to help heal Earth itself — as they seek ALL THINGS GREAT AND SMALL. Interconnected with Animalscape, these two networks are *SOURCE* which elevate the planet to its next level of ascension."

I am feeling wonderment and joy — that animals and children have found one another at this 'time'! And suddenly, I don't know why, legends I remember reading tumble into my mind in such detail that I see them:

> And on a certain day as he was passing by a mountain side nigh unto the desert, there met him a lion and many men were pursuing him with stones and javelins to slay him.
>
> But *Jesus* rebuked them, saying, Why hunt ye these creatures of God, which are more noble than you? By the cruelties of many generations they were made the enemies of man who should have been his friends.
>
> If the power of God is shewn in them, so also is shewn his long suffering and compassion. Cease ye to persecute this creature who desireth not to harm you; see ye not how he fleeth from you, and is terrified by your violence?
>
> And the lion came and lay at the feet of Jesus, and showed love to him; and the people were astonished, and said, Lo, this man loveth all creatures and hath power to command even these beasts from the desert, and they obey him.[3]
>
> And as *Jesus* was going to Jericho there met him a man with a cage full of birds which he had caught and some young doves. And he saw how they were

in misery having lost their liberty, and moreover being tormented with hunger and thirst.

And he said unto the man, What doest thou with these? And the man answered, I go to make my living by selling these birds which I have taken.

And *Jesus* said, What thinkest thou, if another, stronger than thou or with greater craft, were to catch thee and bind thee, or thy wife, or thy children, and cast thee into a prison, in order to sell thee into captivity for his own profit, and to make a living?

Are not these thy fellow creatures, only weaker than thou? And doth not the same *God our Father-Mother* care for them as for thee? Let these thy little brethren and sisters go forth into freedom, and see that thou do this thing no more, but provide honestly for thy living.

And the man marvelled at these words and at his authority, and he let the birds go free. So when the birds came forth they flew unto *Jesus* and stood on his shoulder and sang unto him.

And the man inquired further of his doctrine, and he went his way, and learnt the craft of making baskets, and by this craft he earned his bread and afterwards he brake his cages and his traps, and became a disciple of *Jesus*.[4]

Direct Connection With Shamanic Essence

I'm now in a place where I can see the great contribution, through the 'ages' and cultures, of shamanic visionaries. These understandings bring the view that the Universe is constantly changing within life's flow. To be within that flow we must be willing to constantly let go of everything.

Hindu religion purports it is *Shiva** who represents this flow of life, and is known as *Lord of the Dance.** It is his dance that keeps the Universe in motion. As we let go of what no longer serves we also release all that is impure and excessive. But I see that greater civilization does not understand these concepts, and so it is that physical waste is only accumulated . . . as in pollution of the planet and surrounding hemispheres, even to the point that Earth is ostracized and condemned at large within the Universe.

As I am watching this heavy surrounding fog, I am suddenly filled with a sense of peace and connectedness with *Mother Earth* — realizing that into my presence has come a *Great Being* who sits before me, legs crossed and eyes downcast. I see that he is Native American, here to offer me a lost message. He speaks slowly and deliberately, with the wisdom of Earth herself but from a place of higher knowledge and truth. . . .

"The **HOPI PROPHECY SEEKERS**, known as **Great Elders**, wish to be represented here, offering awarenesses which eliminate pollution within spheres surrounding Earth.

"Removal of this waste is being accomplished as we speak, within the visionary work of **THE WHITE BROTHERHOOD*** and **THE MELCHIZEDEKS**.* As this higher clearing is completed, it needs to be accomplished in physical reality as well. The *Hopis'* search takes them to coils of higher technologies which emanate forth to open up the readership to higher possibilities for the clearing needed.

"As you feel this source of *spiralling* down, planetary consciousness* aligns with the truths of the *Great Elders*, and Earth begins to clear itself. All pollution expands and then dissolves within itself by virtue of its seeking dissolution! These truths manifest completely . . . but the planet needs to work toward its own clearing, on other levels of consciousness. Through this work, humanity is able to purge itself of the fog which has surrounded Earth."

The Elder vanishes in billowing smoke, and I am filled with humility and gratitude for these words offered by One who sees the greater good, and seeks only to share that knowledge. . . .

And as I am smugly thinking I've now seen and heard it all, a most spectacular blinding light bursts forth and I'm again overcome by the overwhelming presence of the MASTER OF LOVE Himself, here in full view, first as He is initially on Earth — and now as She is here within GODDESS energy to validate Earth for its expansion!

CHRIST CONSCIOUSNESS OF THE SECOND COMING* emanates into the bookscape with three messages of higher counsel:

First, is the importance of a more highly elevated lifestyle on a regular, ongoing basis, within One's relationships and day to day living. SOURCE offers the ability to co-create exactly what One seeks, through heightened use of telepathy between beings on Earth, and between Earth and higher dimensions. As the veil continues to lift, dimensional shifting becomes more viable and thought forms materialize. Therefore with this heightened ability, One's thoughts are of highest importance!

Second, is the need for a belief system with a solid foundation of trust and faith which allows opening up depths of self to higher trust, faith and knowingness that *SOURCE* itself flows through **CHRIST CONSCIOUSNESS.** *The Arcturian Sisterhood as wayshowers* speak as *ONE* when they affirm these truths and validate emanation of **CHRIST COMING** into ALL THINGS GREAT AND SMALL, thus culminating in Earth's exponential purification and expansion.

Third, is a message from All Intergalactic beingness* within this universe and beyond, that they emanate from *SOURCE,* as does humanity, and their cellular structure and realities are yours. At this 'time' they offer support in the global expansion; these higher beings wait to be seen and acknowledged by humanity as other Earthly beingness has done, but this cannot happen until there is readiness to open up at higher levels.

Messages completed, the great light appears to expand as it *spirals* upward and outward into the Universe . . . and I am left experiencing only a deep sense of the perfection of ALL THINGS. In the aftermath come deeper understandings of what is:

I see the work of healers affirmed over and over as they seek higher *love* for themselves and others. I see that for coming events to happen, enough self individuation has to occur on all levels of the psyche, for both animals and humans. This higher and deeper expansion of truth is the direct connection to **CHRIST CONSCIOUSNESS**, completing the *DIVINE* connective system of highways. The infrastructure is then able to support *SPIRIT'S* Plan for ALL THINGS GREAT AND SMALL. Oh, how grand is the *DIVINE PLAN!!!*

MAGNIFICENT SHIFTS

And it is with this deepened understanding and sense of joy that I return to the continuing panorama of duality. . . .

Just when I feel I can't take any more of this nightmare — the wonderful parts are wonderful, but the inhumanity, the insensitivity, the lack of mercy — sometimes beyond bearing — just when I feel in the center of a good/evil tug of war . . . IT happens.

Lovely, incredible GAIA* cuts loose. . . . There are tornadoes, floods, hurricanes, droughts, earthquakes, tidal waves, higher winds. Upheaval everywhere. GOD is sending rotation needed for Earth to move out of orbit into the cosmos to make a major leap. Rotating into this stratosphere, the skies come alive with inert energies — those which have been stored without use for trillions of

'eons' in order to move Earth to higher *space*. . . .
Incredible happenings!

And I am reminded of **RONAR's** predictions of
remarkable change to come, his *love* for all animals, and
the goal of upliftment of Animal Kingdom. As I think these
thoughts, **RONAR's** magnificent presence fills *spaces*
around me once more.

"You really <u>are</u> serious about ALL this, aren't you?"

"No, but I will introduce you to One who is. This is
RUSTINOR, *High Sirian Connection* between Animalscape
and Earthscape."

"Greetings. I am **RUSTINOR** of *Sirius Star System*."

"Really, it's an honor to meet you. I didn't mean . . . yes,
I see, <u>serious</u>. (I find myself giggling again.) Never mind.
Ah, since you're here, is it possible for you to answer some
questions about these 'latest' things I'm seeing that I don't
quite understand. I mean, if you have . . . well . . . 'time'."

"<u>Are you serious?</u>" (They say in unison.)

(I look from One to the other, and shake my head.) I
must say I'm surprised at all the humor here.

RONAR: "*GOD* invented it, and we have been close to *SOURCE* for some 'time'. It rubs off."

(I have to smile.) "Well, here's the thing. While I'm experiencing all this, I'm communicating my observations to anyone listening. So, anything you can tell me goes straight to them — and maybe it will help us understand what's happening, since things are heating up on Earth."

RUSTINOR: "But that isn't supposed to happen for millions of 'years.'" (She and RONAR are looking at each other innocently.)

"What do you mean?"

RONAR: "The sun burning up Earth."

"No, no. . . . Heating up? No, I mean things are —"

(They are laughing.)

"Oh, I can see where this is going!" (What can I say? Humor obviously knows no bounds.)

RUSTINOR: "We apologize. We have digressed enough. Of course we'll help. You probably know by now there are many beings around us . . . who will speak whenever appropriate."

(In a flash there <u>is</u> another being in front of me.)

"I am **TOPHEZ** of *The Pleiadian Sisterhood*,* to let you know that we send our Spirituality to Earth through a process of beaming and scanning, as in what you know as REIKI. We are the first star system to use this method of connecting to Earth. *The Pleiades* is also served by our connection with your planet, in that *as we serve you, we are also served.*"

"*The Pleiades.* Wow! Yes — I understand the mutual benefit of such a relationship, where, as the saying goes within REIKI practice that *you receive the session which you give.* . . . Thank you, **TOPHEZ!**"

(She is gone as quickly as she arrived.)

"All the 'time' in 3rd Dimension—and I never had a clue about how expansive ALL this is. I feel so . . . dense."

RUSTINOR: "But you are not, in reality. And part of 3rd Dimension's plan, as you see, is the very <u>not</u> <u>knowing</u> of ALL THINGS — but the opportunity, while in physical form to open up to as much as One is willing to <u>see</u>, <u>hear</u>, <u>feel</u>, <u>sense</u> and <u>know</u>."

"Yes . . . yes. . . . I see that's so true. Now, I think I'd like to know more about the connection between humans and *nature* that was lost so 'long ago.' It seems a vital part of what's happening."

RONAR: "*Nature* Kingdom validates your *love* and we take you inside this realm . . . to show you in depth what is occurring in this 'time' you are observing on Earth — during the *shifts of great magnitude*."

"Good, good, I want to understand ALL of it."

RONAR: "First, you should know that *LOVE IS NOT AN ILLUSION*. It is reality seen through the eyes of **GOD/ GODDESS**. Earth is beginning to elevate, but animals are not yet speaking to people — at a high level. While there are some animals who understand humans, fewer humans understand animals. As you watch humanity evolve, you will see more high level interspecies exchange."

RUSTINOR: "Animals such as the dolphins are watching from other dimensions. They operate from 18[th,] and are on Earth in form both to help people move into the animal world, and to evolve animals. *They enable huge shifts which are done both in physicality — and in inner spiritual work.*

"Dolphins are waiting for humanity to seek *love* at their level. Spirituality has to unfold further before the Dolphin Phenomenon* can take effect. Earth's intentional higher makeover also makes over animals — so that they can operate with better acceptance of the chaos and confusion during the transition 'time'."

"What's this Dolphin Phenomenon?? Did I miss something <u>else</u>?"

RONAR: "Simultaneous 'time' notwithstanding, the Phenomenon occurs at a 'future point' in linear reality. Dolphin Phenomenon is the communication (messages) to Animalscape from the dolphins which happens when ALL THINGS GREAT AND SMALL connect at higher and deeper levels with **CHRIST CONSCIOUSNESS**. In the form of signals from the deep, the messages are heard by humanity as well. This is unprecedented in its impact in that ALL form a link together for 'future' realities of a higher *nature*."

"Ohhhhhh!! So, what you're really telling me is that I'm missing out on a phenomenal event!"

RONAR: "<u>You</u> are a phenomenal event!"

"Why thank you, **RONAR** . . . I think. However, I <u>know</u> I'm feeling good about this extraordinary linking of animals and humans."

RONAR: "Exactly so. . . . And all *vegetation* and *elements* are also linked to be Spiritual messengers. ALL THINGS on Earth come from higher truth, and from that *SOURCE* emanates Earth's state of surrealism and beauty — to levels beyond human consciousness. Perhaps you wish to hear some of this on a more personal note?"

"Oh, definitely. I would! I've already heard from Samantha and the trees, and it has just whetted my appetite for more!"

RONAR: "Very well. Allow me to begin with *the skies:* Seeking the skies and their beauty opens up greater truth — as One takes in their sumptuousness and elevated *spaces* — coming to you each 'day' through simply an upward glance. . . .

"Now, do you see the gull? *The seagull* seeks to awaken humanity's consciousness through rotating into *spaces* where teaching is nonexistent. Within its *spiralling* up and down between sky and sea, the gull brings together these realities so they can offer combined essences to Earthscape at large. The gull manifests its truth inside the ocean floor as it seeks sacredness in ALL THINGS. The gull swoops high and low and instills wisdom at universal levels."

(I watch as gull meets *ocean*, and I have that familiar merging feeling that I am part of both.)

RONAR: "And as Earth is realizing beginning *shifting*, birds at large are rotating into the process sooner than other aspects. Birds offer trees the role-modeling of possibilities, seen from higher *Birdscape*. Treescape receives validation from the beauty of Skyscape.* The synergistic effect of this interaction places new validation on each — trees, birds, skies. . . . ALL are *interconnected*."

RUSTINOR: "*Wildflowers* are the shamanic gift, and through rotation into *soil* these creatures of beauty and consciousness take *secret spaces* into Earth. Within hemispheric conditions they can then be received by receptive animals, insects and elements.

"Since *soil* is connected to inner Earth where Spirituality is in its purist state, *soil* is able to offer this truth to the roots of flowers as it offers the bloom to desirers of beauty and love.

"*Wildflowers* seek *love* through being honored for their beauty and sanctification . . . but they also surrender to being picked and offered to others — who are open to their strength and perfection. Their manifestation is a *Godsend*, in order to gift Earth with consciousness of purity and validation of higher beauty and truth."

(I feel myself moving gently with a breeze, smell my fragrances floating through the air . . . and am truly inspired by the brilliant colors. . . . "Please continue," I hear myself saying — from this surreal *space*.)

RONAR: "*The groundhog* not only takes within seasonal changes through its inner knowledge of 'time' aspects of *Creation*, but also takes *extraterrestrial sense**** within! The groundhog senses ALL Spirituality through its connections with soil and inner Earth where realization of higher essence predominates."

(*Soil* feels damp and wonderful around my body — or am I *soil*? Wow!)

RONAR: "*The whip-poor-will* calls to each being on Earth — in its secret reality — where it seeks *love* from all who listen. ALL manifestation looks for a source of connectedness within the context of daily living, but the whip-poor-will calls out to Earthscape to seek higher truth. As Earth begins its <u>leap,</u> the birds call out to begin listening for *GOD* signs,* so *secrets* can be instilled into the very structure of ALL.

"Earth scene opens up these signs and then validates their essence within itself. Signs continue to manifest, and birds On High take them to each species."

"I never would have guessed all this was going on beneath the surface. . . . I could tell things were changing sometime 'before' I got here, but I had no idea. . . . I had no idea. . . ."

RUSTINOR: "Knowledge which animals bring to Earth takes linear *spaces* to new heights as *DIVINE PLAN* keeps the flame warm for ALL beings. Animals make great noises and embrace the coming events with validation and understanding."

"And I see that many humans are searching for deeper ways to connect with forms of consciousness other than their own. I suspect you and others I've been meeting play a part in getting messages out to certain people to pass on to others. I <u>like</u> this scenario!"

RUSTINOR: "We are extremely exuberant over this turn of events. You may be surprised to know that Earth is the first planet to make such a significant comeback. We honor you — and the millions all over the planet — humans and animals — who in seeking their *secret spaces,* raise the vibrational level of Earth itself, in order for these *momentous shifts* to occur."

"I remember feeling more hopeful toward the 'end/beginning', but I wasn't clear what was happening. Now, as I observe the whole picture, it all fits perfectly."

RUSTINOR: "You are among those who heard *the call* that poured in from all over the Universe, perhaps in the form of cheerleading chants — to support, guide, encourage, admonish and alert — *and to do your own inner work!"*

"Yes, yes, I could feel it, but I had no idea! What else, what else?"

RONAR: "Yet another scenario that may surprise you. Scottish *lore* teaches that it is Lassie who comes home to her master — at all costs to herself. But the reality is that Lassie — in essence — never leaves home; only in body does she leave her person. The truth is that the animal who bonds to someone stays with that person — on a Spiritual level — for their mutual 'lifetime'."

"Who would have guessed these connections go this far. . . . *THE DIVINE PLAN* is indeed wide and deep!"

"It is a lot to take in, we realize. . . . Shall we go on?"

"Absolutely."

RONAR: "Lest it be forgotten, the *bumblebee* buzzes round seeking sweet things on Earth — in order to place value on life's sweetness and honey, and to reveal that inside ALL THINGS are found Spiritual truth. From the inside view comes the true picture. . . . The *bumblebee* buzzes through life in industrious manner, and serves Earthscape in a visible and elevated fashion. The *bee* takes GODspaces within its understandings and offers them to other insects who wish to be transformed into higher beings within GOD'S Plan for ALL THINGS."

"How did I miss ALL this interconnectedness?"

RUSTINOR: "Perhaps you did not look in between, or see things in perspective. But again, ALL is in the 'present.' You are not missing this!"

"Yes, I see. . . . I do."

RONAR: ". . . Speaking of being in perspective, may we introduce you to another friend? This is **MORSTEW**, speaking for herself, emanating from the *Web of Life*."

"Oh my." (You're going to *love* this.)

"I am **MORSTEW**, the spider who offers you a higher perspective of insect reality, to help enlighten you as to the deeper meaning of insects. . . .

"Spider webs take Earth substance and transform it into beauty of evolved beingness. As they can, webs take *lore* to higher *spaces*, and *transmute* it to *love*. Intricacies of the web take the labyrinth to new levels — as we weave our work to seek visible truth. Manifestation of truth within the web takes Earthscape to the beauty of higher meaning.

"We spiders are shy creatures — who only bite to save ourselves from being trapped in a corner. Our higher role is in intricate weaving into eternity of Earth substances — in order to create art-like manifestations of higher energetic Creation."

"Oh, I get it! One could say that spiders are artistic weavers, not to mention their required skill to . . . err . . . quickly re-group and begin again!!"

RONAR: "Indeed. I might add here that spider-like beings which manifest the web are also *planetary expansionists,** in that they are drawn to spaces which seek their truths."

MORSTEW: "We thank you, **RONAR!** . . . Our spider consciousness also seeks to heal animals, as we place truth within ALL THINGS. As webs are created and re-created, each web manifests truth into *spaces* where it is located, and this energetic propulsion helps open up *secret spaces* for any being *in the vicinity of the web site.*"

(Humans obviously do not have the corner on subtle humor here.)

"I appreciate your insights, **MORSTEW,** and I'll bet my friends in 3rd Dimension will never mindlessly sweep away another web! I am honored to have met you. I'm really beginning to see how ALL THINGS work together for the greater good."

(A shimmering, colossal-sized web, with **MORSTEW** in it, evaporates before me.)

"Wow!"

RONAR: "And speaking of insights, get ready for this one: *Healing of One individual insect takes the <u>entire</u> consciousness of that species to a higher level. The intention should be for <u>any</u> species. Known as <u>healing of the one</u>,** this concept applies to the Animal Kingdom as well.

"Actively seek *love* for animals and insects. As you walk the daily walk, expect to do healing work as you encounter any individual animal or insect. . . . As *love* is sought within these conditions, it will be realized that animals and insects are seeking healing. As humans are ready to receive them, I offer specific techniques to use in this global healing process.

"And now, let us continue to elevate our sights — within the Insect Kingdom . . . with the *butterfly.* . . . *The butterfly* rotates into higher realities than other insects, and other beings of light at this 'time.' In its ability to transform itself through complete and total rejuvenation into another state of physicality, the *butterfly* is able to offer *secret spaces* to the Universe at large . . . for the transformation of ALL who will receive its truth.

"The *butterfly* can show ALL manifestation the connection between dimensions. In its fluttering about, it offers the illusory beingness which flows into the consciousness of the fortunate beholder . . . thus allowing movement between dimensions of inner worlds.

"Often sacrificed by misled humans in order to display its beauty, the *butterfly* is only able to be beautiful in its living state where it does its work and makes the transformation to another dimension."

(As I am hearing this, a lovely quote I've never forgotten flutters through my mind: *"Once upon a time, I, Chuang Tzŭ,*[5] *dreamt I was a butterfly, fluttering hither and thither, unconscious of my individuality as a man. Suddenly, I awaked, and there I lay, myself again. Now I do not know whether I was then a man dreaming I was a butterfly, or whether I am now a butterfly, dreaming I am a man."*)

I hear **RUSTINOR** and **RONAR** communicating to me from somewhere but suddenly I — oh my — am light as a feather in the wind. . . . I . . . have . . . wings. How exhilarating to smell and taste the sweetness inside this flower. I hear my new friends asking if I am okay. . . . Oh yes. . . . I'm just fine! Please go on. . . . I continue to flit . . . from bloom to bloom . . . in a field of brilliantly colored wildflowers . . . feeling the warmth of sun and the smell of Earth . . . can you feel the wings? . . . and the wind helps me float . . . feel the wings. . . .

RUSTINOR: "That is indeed a tribute to this noble insect being. And speaking of winged Ones, let us tell of *the* geese . . . who take reality into their *sacred spaces* and convert it into truth. Uniquely able to find *GOD* on Earth, geese find answers for themselves <u>within</u> themselves. They wait for Animal Kingdom to query them for solutions, as they take responsibility for sacredness to a higher level than other animals."

"One thing that I am noticing in this early part of the *shifts* is that the predator instinct still seems to be alive and well within Animal Kingdom, with animals eating other animals."

RONAR: "Ah. . . . Carnivorous animals still eating other life forms? They do not yet understand that higher truth does not validate this condition, but as you see, they manifest higher understanding within 'future.' It begins in small numbers within each species, so the word can be spread amongst the entire species through modeling of changed behavior."

"Amazing."

RONAR: "This is happening on other levels. Animal structural integration* (inner strength and inner sanctity before *GOD*) is elevating itself through actual changes in DNA make-up. Through use of *The 100ᵗʰ Monkey Concept** the more highly evolved animals within each species are seeking this elevated state of consciousness, and offering its reality to others.

"As if by magic, they are transforming themselves. This structural process takes about twenty 'years' of Earth 'time', but you see how animals are preparing for the gradual *transmutation* — and how humans are offering healing techniques to manifest and support ALL this."

(*The healing techniques*, of which I was only vaguely aware, blazon across the sky in huge letters!)

THE EYES HAVE IT: instills healing through your inner realization of higher consciousness and your ability to EYEBALL the animal and send it greater self love. This technique releases the animal from the entrapment experienced within Earthly dimensionality and facilitates a shift into 6th Dimensional consciousness. The format is the initial presence with the animal, the receiving of information from the animal through One's intuition, and the sending of healing as needed. There is a mutuality of sending and receiving, as you wait for your own inner guidance to know about the animal's inner needs.

Healing is achieved as human and animal consciousnesses merge — and a true soul connection is established between you and the animal. Through the mutuality of the eyeballing experience, dimensions blend and cross over, and the animal surrenders to a greater understanding. As this occurs, there is a synergistic healing effect for both animal and human.

SEEDING: used to comfort and protect an abused animal who is being housed or sheltered from harm, but who appears to have acclimated to its surroundings, for example, an animal in foster care or in a sanctuary. The technique is begun with use of The Eyes, but then the focus moves to expanding the animal's consciousness. Place your hands on the animal and seed it with your intention that it feel safe and protected, focusing on elevating its consciousness to higher truth.

This process cannot always be done in physicality. One can simply visualize the animal's soul and then telepath a higher realization of a safe and secure setting. The technique offers an abused animal a perspective beyond that of Earthly realities; through your touch it feels more secure and connected to a higher Godliness.

ALTERING ESSENCES OF SOUL: used with a distraught, highly vulnerable and upset animal, for example, a dog that is constantly kept chained outside. An altered state of consciousness helps the animal find higher soul essence and is achieved through the following stages:

A. Get the animal's attention through a form of speaking, toning, or use of gentle touching if appropriate;

B. Move the animal to an altered state of consciousness through your intention using The Eyes Technique, or through spiralling the animal inward with a pendulum, or other instrument. This then allows the animal to experience and internalize a higher state of Godliness to help counter the effects of Earthly abuse;

C. Ground the animal's consciousness back to Earth by placing One's hands on its body, if possible. This helps the animal bring back the healing visualization to this plane and to incorporate it into its psyche. Take this step with caution; if a wild animal, be aware of its limited tolerance for touch;

D. Reinforce the animal's heightened reality through stroking its fur or surface in such a way as to convey love and caring. This technique works with insects and all Earth consciousness, even stones and soil, as they become disrupted through the force of human construction and destruction;

E. Repeat this entire healing technique periodically, if possible, in order to offset previous abuse and to help the animal foster and develop a new or renewed trust in humanity and Earthly consciousness. (Note: all these stages can be accomplished through One's intention when the use of physical touch is not appropriate.)

TRANSITION: offers healing to the soul of an animal in transition from Earth to another plane. This can be done through One's simple intention, in the form of prayer or sending healing energies or thoughts. The animal consciousness is seeking love as it takes its soul manifestation from Earth to another plane where it will receive love on all levels. The overall focus is simply to have the intention to place the animal in higher spaces.

For a deceased animal (for example, by the roadside) One can offer the following affirmation or prayer: May the soul of this animal be in its right and perfect place, and may any negative energies still surrounding the body be replaced with light, love, healing and harmony.

(As if these Techniques are not enough in themselves, I am astounded as **RONAR** flashes across my vision, surpassing even himself in his role as Top Dog!)

RONAR: "I am manifesting in this 'moment' as Dog ON HIGH, within the human psyche. I offer a *special implant**to humans — for the asking — that places *secret spaces* within animals. Simply invoke my presence at any 'time.' Through this implant, *love* manifests within the animal soul. It can then be used by individuals or large groups of humans at once — to heal and serve a single animal or small group of animals. This technique offers animals the benefit of human condition at a higher level of functioning."

(Sigh) . . . "As wonderful as ALL this is, I'm feeling quite chagrined because I'm realizing that I wasn't paying a lot of attention before I got here. It would have made the rest of the 'time' in 3rd Dimension a lot richer."

RUSTINOR: "But you are here, and there is no 'time,' so you are experiencing it all NOW."

"Tell me I'll get used to this . . . that I won't constantly be slipping back."

"ALL is perfect in this 'time' and place. Fear not."

"I'm relieved to hear that, believe me."

RONAR: "Let us work on it together."

"Wonderful."

"In this 'time' of *shifting* vibrational level you are viewing, humans who are open to higher vibration can encounter any animal and send *love* through their eyes. At the same 'time,' they receive *love* from the animal's eyes. *This love expands exponentially from human to animal, from animal to human* — as ripples in a pond. . . . And speaking of the ripple effect. . . ."

RUSTINOR: "The *springlike essence* of Earth's soil comes from *Deep Waters of ALL THINGS*, beneath the cold calmness of Earth's surface. Falling of water is falling of realities to new and fresh springlike expression of *GOD*. Inner *springs* are still pure and unpolluted, and remain so by hiding within Earth's formation.

"Planetary movement takes *springs* into ways to find inner truth, and to offer this reality to other formations at levels of vibration not known to humanity or animals at large. Animals find underground, spring-like activity as they seek Spirit, but it is also instilled in their essence, as they run in the woods, forests and wilderness.

"As *springs of Earth* keep flowing, animals take heart in knowing that Earthscape will one day reach that level of purity. Underground *springs* elevate to higher truth in spite of their position which appears to be at the bottom of Earth. . . ."

"Err, wasn't it **JESUS** who actually said appearances are not always what they seem . . . and the lowly shall become the GODLY ?"

RONAR and **RUSTINOR** (in unison): "*As the spring of eternal wisdom manifests within Animal Kingdom, it also emanates forth into the world, so that ALL beings are able to see its magnificence. Truth is found inside ALL beings in some small manifestation, but the spring within Earthscape manifests in fullness ALL the goodness of GOD — and offers these understandings as Earth is ready to receive them.*"

RONAR: "With your permission, let us keep moving, as there is much to cover yet . . . but we must move quickly from greatest depths to greatest heights. I am now proud to introduce you to **SHEBAT**, a *Tibetan High Dog.*"

"**SHEBAT**, *What an honor* to meet you." (A dog from Tibet. . . . This should be good. I'm ready, are you?)

"I greet you as well. Dogs of Tibet are found on Earth for only one reason: to seek higher truth within ALL THINGS

GREAT AND SMALL. We seek *love* in highest forms available for animal consciousness. Know that Earth is impacted as we speak, in that Tibetan dogs live GOD'S *Word*.

"We take *love* to new levels, but, like all animals, need connection to the human touch, to our particular person. Our genetic 'history' brings us to the present state of consciousness wherein we seek only the integrity of our structural spiritual process. We offer new ways to interact with animals, and bring new awarenesses as to coming events.

"*It is the connection to our persons which offers a cord of higher truth.* * Within **CHRIST CONSCIOUSNESS** *it emanates from Heaven to Earth in silver and gold tones of elevated spaces. Higher consciousness is achieved as the emerging cord flows into Earth and offers its prototype* * *to be sought within the meditative state.*"

"I'm <u>so moved</u> by this, and honored by your presence, **SHEBAT**. You are truly a blessing to ALL Earthscape at this 'time'."

"It is <u>I</u> who am honored."

(Just when I expect there to be more interaction, this gracious being melts into the magnificent mountains that surround us.)

"RUSTINOR, RONAR, can you continue?? I see 'time' seeming to speed up on the planet. I remember that frenzied feeling. What's happening?"

RONAR: "Masters through the 'ages', as you have witnessed, seek higher truth but are unable to find it on Earth. But now Earth is making over into spaces where *DIVINE* love is available to ALL seekers."

RUSTINOR: *"The Lamb of GOD* found in the Bible as JESUS, is not only human, but is also the true connection between humanity and the Animal Kingdom. This is the missing link which humanity has not understood. Animals understand the blessed connection between themselves and humanity, but are limited because of what humanity seeks. What you are witnessing is the beginning of* **The Event of The Second Coming.** *CHRIST CONSCIOUSNESS will manifest true connection — for all who have eyes to see."*

"This is all so extraordinary . . . going on right under my nose. Where was I?"

"Know that these <u>are</u> extraordinary 'times'. You — like so many — have been hampered by limited beliefs but were/are waking up in different ways . . . but <u>awakening</u> nonetheless!"

"Thank you for being kind. Though I have the feeling there is more I missed, am missing." (They look at each other knowingly.) "Go ahead . . . please."

RUSTINOR: "As we have left **SHEBAT** in the high country of Tibet, we continue with our story in other high places. The mountainside is used for vegetation and growing, and seeks higher elevation through **CHRIST**'s teachings. As the mountain opens up to higher extraterrestrial civilizations, let us go to another story. . . .
"*Sirian higher truth teaches that* **CHRIST** *does not come to Earth to realize his crucifixion, but to offer humankind truth. The Animal Kingdom knows . . . that* **CHRIST CONSCIOUSNESS** *waits for higher answers through use of altered states.**"

"Excuse me, **RUSTINOR**, but what's this about *altered states?* Sounds like hypnosis, or something. . . ."

"*Validate that* **JESUS** *uses altered states to reach a higher plane where the love that he seeks is transmuted* directly into Earthscape. His Spirituality validates the technique of hypnotherapy* using sub and super-conscious minds. As old energies are released, secret spaces are consciously realized, and healing and new learning occurs. Termed soul retrieval* within higher Sirian consciousness, it is viewed as a means to Spiritual growth and is suggested for animals as well as humans."

"Who would have thought of hypnotherapy as higher truth . . . as a way of healing and evolving new consciousness?"

"Validate that this therapy comes directly from earliest techniques in medicine where the physician of 'old' hypnotizes the patient in order to provide higher relaxation and serenity. What is not yet understood on Earth is that One's subconscious mind connects to the entire biosphere of the planet and can be accessed with one hundred percent accuracy . . . as **CHRIST CONSCIOUSNESS** teaches within ALL THINGS GREAT AND SMALL."

RONAR: "Well, Rusty, do you think it's time to teach at the graduate level?"

RUSTINOR: (smiling). "You must mean shamanic visionary zoological study. . . ."

(I gulp and smile, because I'm feeling that this is already well beyond the graduate level of learning. . . . However, I dare not stop now. . . .)

RONAR: "At this 'time,' I would offer you use of *shamanic visionary zoological elevation.** Don't be put off by the name! It is done within the process of meditation. Invoke the image of a specific animal within your empathic vision, and with the image in mind, open up healing within yourself by simply seeking healing of the animal.

"This technique can apply to a universal level of animal species, such as the snakes, cats, dogs, elephants . . . and as a synergistic effect is realized, a joint healing occurs within both human and animal states."

"Amazing! It again validates connectedness between species, in that joint healing is accomplished!"

RUSTINOR: "Animals already understand the healing value of this process, both for them and for Earth consciousness as well. And it can be done in the comfort of One's home."

"Oh my gosh! I suddenly understand what **TEDSTRE** was getting at 'earlier'!" (Before I have 'time' to finish the thought, a being appears, greeting all of us, then directing her words to me.)

"I am **ALTIRIA** of *Sirian Sisterhood* and have come at **TEDSTRE**'s request to finish what she began, but which seemed quite boggling at the 'time.' It will now fit easily into your knowingness."

"Thank you, **ALTIRIA**, and please thank **TEDSTRE** for being so patient with my first attempts at understanding. I'm feeling more ready to take ALL this in."

ALTIRIA: "*Greater planetary zoological arena,** which **TEDSTRE** mentioned 'earlier', refers to The Intergalactic Confederation of All Higher Consciousness which exists in form within the greater picture, and includes Amphibia and Tri-lateral beings not known to humanity until this 'time.'

"These represent greater dimensionality not yet embraced as humanity's 'origin' and 'future', within ALL THINGS GREAT AND SMALL. But as global expansion continues, manifestations from this arena enter consciousness and offer high realities, truths and support for global expansion. This includes not only extraterrestrial beings described in *lore*, but other forms not known at this 'time.' They seek further discovery as we meet for 'future' discussions."

"'*Future*' discussions?? You mean there is <u>even more</u>?"

"Without question, we have only just begun!"

(I look at **RONAR** and **RUSTINOR**, knowing smiles lighting them up once more. Meanwhile, **ALTIRIA** disappears in a flash, before I can thank her again.)

"Might we get back to the mountainside you were speaking of? I'm so blown away by all this . . . extraterrestrial expansion stuff that a mountainside sounds rather comfortable, don't you think?"

(They maintain placid expressions — not at all perturbed by my ramblings and continued ignorance.)

RUSTINOR: "The mountainside story resumes from higher realities with the revelation that animals are now able to receive knowledge of their Earthly bond with humans, to heal together within the process of global expansion. This is happening now in grand manner!

"Rotation into mountainside depths takes you to higher truths resounding outward to your ears, offering deeper realities. Openings to *GOD* found *inside the mountain itself* were placed there by **JESUS**, while speaking to the people of Israel. . . .

"At soul level, understand that *spaces* within the mountain are found within Earth's soil. As animals feel the touch of soil, they sense Earth's Spirituality within their structure. Earth structure mirrors the internal structure of every being, and replicates animal and human structure — and vice versa. Each emulates the other and emulates Universe at large, at cellular levels. Everything exists in proportion to everything else and ALL THINGS mirror each other in form. ALL THINGS come from the same *SOURCE* and are made in emulation of *SOURCE* itself. As animals wait for structural integration to occur, they place these truths within humanity. . . ."

RONAR: "This Spiritual knowledge is received by animals in Interlife experience, where they are validated as truth seekers. Individual animals may find *GOD* inside their structure through connection to their person. As the animal manifests this *love* in its own reality, it can then manifest it to other seekers, including vegetation and soil."

"But, **RONAR**, what about the fact that animals are still eating other animals? Is this not reflective of *lore* rather than *love*?"

(**RONAR** patiently goes on): "The animal continues to eat other realities through its conditions of old, of which we have spoken. It is seeking to be fed through the *lore* of Earthspaces, rather than looking upward. The answer for animals is found in humanity's higher Spirituality rather than in current conditions.

"As human Spirit evolves, animals likewise manifest Spiritual growth. As humanity finds opportunities for healing animals, <u>there is a joint healing process that develops</u>."

"I am speechless." (You may find this difficult to believe, but I really am.)

"I am **RUSTINOR** . . . offering you this reassurance of Animal Kingdom's readiness for **THE CHRIST COMING**, and assurances that signs manifest for animals at the right 'times' and places — so they seek truth more fully on Earth.

"Let animals know that all is well on Earth and in Heaven as we speak, through day to day conversations. Use of this communication, both verbally and through telepathy, between humans and animals is a function of the healing process. These understandings give animals hope for co-existence — for sharing of Earth in compatibility and *love* for each other — as has been foretold."

"**RONAR**, I'm awestruck by the trust which animals place in humanity, in their willingness to put themselves in the same spaces with humans, in a position of submission and complete vulnerability. Animals must have great faith in DIVINE PLAN for Earth. How are they able to make this leap of faith? . . . And are Animals in charge of their own destinies? Why would they choose to come to Earth at all?"

RONAR: "Ahhh, now you are really getting into the nitty gritty . . . and the answers may surprise you.

"Earth is unique. While animals take charge of their higher realities, here they surrender their realities to the human condition and to human Spirituality. Emanating from the Interlife, this is termed soul contract of surrender.*

"Earth is the only planet where this condition exists, where animals surrender beingness to their human connection — and where reality seeks healing on all levels. Because of this, the healing and shifting process depends on the combined healing of both animals and humans.

"Not only that, but reality which exists on Earth is unique within the history of civilization: the agreement between humans and animals takes healing potential into the highest available concept within form itself. Therefore, its risk is exponential in that if it is not successful, the form concept is forever diminished into lost spaces and the process must begin again within THE HIGHER DIVINE PLAN."

"NOW I am <u>really</u> speechless. . . . So much at stake here . . . I never in my wildest imaginings . . . I had no idea. . . ."

RONAR: "Yes, exactly . . . there is much to be considered here. It is acknowledged that if global interspecies bonding does not occur, Earthly existence will not achieve the soul essence needed to manifest form again on this 3rd level of dimensionality. This will result in major *DIVINE* surgery! The *HIGHER DIVINE PLAN* is for interspecies bonding to happen and for ALL THINGS GREAT AND SMALL to be realized.

"If this does not happen, Earth will lose the benefit of form because form will no longer serve its purpose in being a vehicle for the instilling of truth. And at the point you are observing, this reality is not yet understood because people have not glimpsed ALL THINGS GREAT AND SMALL as a concept. . . ."

"Sooo, the importance of telepathic communication between animals and humans takes on even added significance, in order for humanity to <u>begin</u> to understand animal teachings . . . and the importance of *interspecies bonding!*"

RONAR: "Well understood! You are beginning *to get it,* and the animals rejoice at your awakening!

"You are familiar with the 100th MONKEY PRINCIPLE* mentioned earlier?? Let me refresh you: As the legend is told, there is a female monkey on an island who learns to wash dirt off raw potatoes and teaches this trick to many other receptive monkeys on the island . As the 100th monkey learns to perform this task, an ideological breakthrough occurs: almost every monkey in the tribe learns to wash potatoes before eating them. . . ."

RUSTINOR: "Then a most surprising thing occurs and is observed by scientists: this habit of washing potatoes 'jumps' over the sea. *As if by magic,* monkeys on other islands and on nearby mainland begin washing <u>their</u> potatoes!!! *Thus, when a certain critical number (critical mass) achieves an awareness, it may be communicated from mind to mind. And there is a point at which, if only one more person tunes in to a new awareness, an energy field is strengthened such that this awareness is picked up by almost everyone!"*

RONAR (vibrating very fast): "However, it gets even better. . . . The 100th Monkey Concept is aligned with **THE SECOND COMING OF CHRIST** as higher Earth evolves. *As this* **EVENT** *becomes the new prototype,* * *telepathy* *awakens within consciousness of those who seek higher truth. Telepathy is validated among the few who have eyes to see and ears to hear and is spread among greater realities. Seekers are then able to heal ALL animal and human consciousness.*

"The planet manifests, as you will see, into separate components based on the principle of free will. Those who seek *love* move into light body,* but those who seek *lore* remain within 3rd Dimension where they continue to seek struggle and untruth. As these two <u>potential</u> realities spread apart, there are openings to 4th Dimension — for healing. An *Elevator** remains open to this reality for 'time' space of many 'years', and many ways, to seek higher *love*."

"Wait, wait!! Hold it! I do understand the separate realities. But what's this Elevator thing? Unbelievable — I see it operating right in front of me. And, I see how the 100TH Monkey Principle actually works over the entire planet! How absolutely astonishing that these major *shifts* can occur with nothing but telepathic communication!! But what about the Elevator??"

RUSTINOR: "The Elevator offers ways to ascend and to travel between dimensions . . . as *transmutation* of *secret spaces* evolves within each Spiritual being. The symbol of the elevator is a metaphor for the soul, as bread rises through the use of yeast and warmth. Elevation to truth comes forth within each being of heightened consciousness.

"But structural integration through altered DNA is not complete at this point in 'time.' Thus, many individuals are feeling lost and limbic — because of incomplete transformation. Some feel GOD-forsaken in their attempts to elevate to higher ways."

"Oh, yes! I am seeing it now! The Elevator scenario is like the answer to ALL THINGS, in that as the Elevator moves up and down, *spaces* which seek higher *love* place validation on the movement itself. Growth comes through actual travel, not just through reaching One's destination! In other words, the journeyer is realizing a much broadened reality through understandings of another 'time' and 'space'. . . . Getting there is half the fun!"

RUSTINOR: "Your awarenesses are definitely heightening! You may also note that with this new technology, the body form on Earth is able to transcend linear 'time' and seek *spaces* within other lifetimes or personas. The seeker can then expand existing world view through soul retrieval of lost aspects of self, not to mention expanded abilities now available to do *inner work*.

"As *secret spaces* of **CHRIST CONSCIOUSNESS** are received, each receptive being is able to validate and integrate their sacred essence. And so higher Earth manifests for all seekers. Openings to 5ᵗʰ Dimension appear and are available in greater frequency and realness as *Dimensional shifts* take shape slowly. **CHRIST-LIKE** elevated spaces of 5ᵗʰ Dimension are truth at highest levels of human understanding."

RONAR: *"Spiritual realities are available for ALL manifestation . . . and the Elevator is running at full speed. As each being chooses higher reality, answers to planetary evolvement manifest before GOD. Final manifestation opens Earth to the grandeur of higher animal splendor.* * *Earth manifests into 5ᵗʰ Dimension realities which animals co-create with GOD — by virtue of their Spirituality. This is the Garden of Eden — as it seeks higher love."*

"So here we are, on the brink of the great shifts. I can't believe how exciting it is to experience it all over again. I'm so glad I've had all of you to give such insights. You know, my friends will want the same experience when they find out about this. And perhaps you could give us more details about things we've missed?"

"ALL is possible."

"I see that. I utterly see that."

(As if to underline their statement, a brilliant light manifests before us, and there appears a most phenomenal Angelic Presence.)

"I am **MICHAEL, ARCHANGEL ON HIGH,** placing my rotation into Earthscape so that *secret spaces* of Angelic Presence can manifest for all beings to receive and integrate. My consciousness has been felt by watchers* and waiters* for some 'time,' but as Earth evolves, this angelic essence combines with Earth's Spirituality, so that it is like fog rising."

(**RUSTINOR** and **RONAR** are calmly and serenely taking all this in. I am . . . well . . . you can only imagine. He continues.)

"As *angelic consciousness** appears on Earth, ALL who recognize and honor it are elevated into The Wings of Higher Angelic Presence through their intention. Realities are opened further through the expanding Ascension Process. Angelic Presence on Earth is connection to higher Spirituality as One enters higher states of consciousness, by simply being open to Angelic reality. *As above, so below. . . .*"

(The light flashes and **MICHAEL** is gone. I compose myself as best I can, and see that **RONAR** and **RUSTINOR** are smiling those knowing smiles.)

RUSTINOR: "In this transition 'time,' you also notice there are techniques provided to raise *Godliness Quotient** on Earth — so that the shadow land called Earth emanates forth in light and *love*, and *lore* manifests as *love*. Seeking of Spirituality leads to truth. As humans communicate with *Nature*, they are communing with *GODDESS* Energies and through these energies Earth is moving into the next stage of evolution."

(All three of us share a quiet moment, after which **RUSTINOR** and **RONAR** fade into the myriad of animal beings and surrounding elemental loveliness . . . and everything bursts into a *spiral* of dazzling lights.)

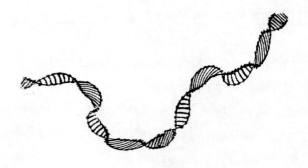

STRUCTURAL INTEGRATION . . . AND NEW HEIGHTS

In the ongoing panorama before me, I see now that as **CHRIST CONSCIOUSNESS** nears, Earth is realizing its approach. As a result, old energies are rising and releasing. As negativity is released, so global realities become more explosive and more gnostic (*GODLINESS*-seeking) so that contrasts become more apparent.

I see that as echoes reverberate individually, interpersonally and internationally, the final implosion takes Earth to places where old realities seek final releasement into the atmosphere. As this occurs, Soul Retrieval of **THE SECOND COMING** begins its expansion into higher *spaces* than have ever been on Earthscape. The final implosion is, in fact, placement of internal restructured DNA within humanity.

Hold that thought for a second, because I do believe that I have finally surpassed myself — yes, I have! Glory be! It has taken all this 'time', even in this place, but I am really starting to see what this whole thing is about. Soul Retrieval, that is. It is not what One would think, not just some silly, esoteric technique. Nor is **CHRIST CONSCIOUSNESS** what One would think:

The Essence of **CHRIST CONSCIOUSNESS** *is being retrieved from within all beingness on Earthscape. WE THE SEEKERS ARE INDEED* **CHRIST CONSCIOUSNESS.**

Are you getting this???

As I am still struggling to grasp <u>this</u> revelation, I realize there is a book . . . yes . . . a book . . . here. By now, in this place, nothing should come as a shock, but this book appears to have the gift of language. . . . One tries to remain open-minded . . . but <u>this</u>!

"I do indeed speak to you, through soul essence of **CHRIST CONSCIOUSNESS.** I, The <u>I-Ching</u>,* seek representation in the bookscape as a perfect replica of DNA. I am the oldest Earthly document known to embrace all higher DNA Structure. Within my pages higher emanation can be viewed, as humanity seeks to evolve and structurally change consciousness everywhere."

"You mean DNA of all consciousness everywhere in all Creation is changing now!??" (Here I am talking to a book and it actually makes sense to me. Give me strength.)

"I do. It may also surprise you that DNA is what surrounds Earth."

"Ohhh. And in order to change my DNA, I need to personally make it happen. . . ."

"Yes. Personal transformation only occurs as One seeks inner change. Here is a personal affirmation for now: 'I allow my spiritual beingness to expand my DNA in order to unfold the ultimate truth!'"

"How appropriate! Thank you."

"The I-Ching's hidden meaning is about to be unlocked as these secret spaces reveal themselves. I, The I-Ching open up the Elevator to higher spaces, for within these pages the DNA Connection itself is stored. Within my riddles is found the sacred base comprising ALL Creation's essence. As DNA expands, exponential growth will occur within all consciousness."

As I take in these final words, the Great Book simply closes itself and disappears from my field of vision . . . just as I begin to formulate some intelligible questions!! What can possibly surpass *this*?? (Dare I ask!)

As there seems to be no end to possibilities in <u>this realm</u>, so the polarities on Earth seem to be at their height of . . . well . . . polarity, at this 'time' I am viewing. And, truthfully, I'm still not understanding their purpose. . . .

"Let me enlighten you further. . . ."

(I see that **RUSTINOR** has indeed returned, but then her shining light is never far away in this place.)

"At this point in 'time', absence of higher truth is still prevalent and Earth is referred to by greater Universal realities as The Zone of Avoidance.* But as **CHRIST CONSCIOUSNESS** shines its light into ALL dark spaces, opportunities open to raise One's soul consciousness. Answers to ALL THINGS manifest as this awakening continues and as DNA is changed through restructuring human condition *and linear reality itself.*

"Polarities of consciousness serve higher truth in that as they separate and pull apart from each other, the process evokes deepening of consciousness such that the DNA

Structure is expanded and restructured, and human essence itself is lightened up."

"I guess I needed that last bit of DNA stuff, because now I get it! Hallelujah!! Oh, yes, I see the emerging human state of heightened consciousness, and that One can now restructure One's essence. And manifesting at a higher level, One can see truth within ALL form."

"You have indeed learned by leaps and bounds! Call on any of us if you need further clarification."

"Thank you, **RUSTINOR.**"
(A mist surrounds me and she is gone.)

It is with mounting joy and anticipation that I sense it all coming together — as Higher Earth itself is restructured. Ah! What rapture I see before me! Humanity is elevating through heightened abilities to *love*, as telepathic awarenesses become general knowledge, and people see animals in higher ways.

The significance of global bonding is being grasped! As the veil lifts, the essence of Higher Earth is glimpsed and joins with the consciousness of seekers. As increasing numbers grasp these greater soul understandings, **CHRIST CONSCIOUSNESS** expands.

INTO THE GARDEN

In the greater panorama of humanity's evolvement, I clearly see little beams of light, constant and undaunted by what swirls around them. I mention these in the spirit of the whole, because I don't wish you to believe that *shifts* come about in one fell swoop — with absolutely nothing to herald their arrival!

I see Albert Schweitzer's beam of light, and Rachel Carson's and Aldo Leopold's, and beams of swirling light from Mohandus Gandhi, Diane Fossey, Galileo, William Shakespeare, Nelson Mandela, George Washington Carver, Jane Goodall, Helen Keller, Pearl Buck, Cesar Chavez, The Dalai Lama, Edgar Cayce, Chuang Tzu, Michelangelo, George Bernard Shaw, Thich Naht Hanh, Alice Walker, Francis of Assisi, Joseph Wood Krutch, Joy Adamson, Henry David Thoreau, J. Allen Boone, Maya

Angelou, Kahlil Gibran, Chief Seattle, Albert Einstein, Leonardo DaVinci, Drunvalo Melchizedek, Richard Bach, Brooke Medicine Eagle, Matthew Fox, Dorothy Maclean, Meister Eckhart, Alick McInnes, former President Cannon of the Church of Latter Day Saints — not to mention all the unsung heroes of high consciousness whose work goes largely unknown — as their little lights shine — in the world at large.

I am seeing more and more *beams of light* from here — there — everywhere on the planet — more and more:

The elderly person is sharing love and meager food with neighborhood dogs; the dogs giving love and comfort in return. . . .

The children cleaning up the stream bed, the vacant city lot, the roadside — creating beauty once again. . . .

A young man remaining true to his Spiritual self despite prejudice, bigotry and his family's betrayal. . . .

The mother cat risking her life, returning again and again to a burning building to save her kittens. . . .

Many, in war-torn countries, choosing not to hate, who do not see themselves as separate from their sisters and brothers of the other side, who pray for peace. . . .

Tibetan refugees, no matter what their poverty and plight, scooping up a mouse in their midst and removing it to a safer place. . . .

Seekers of wisdom and truth who through their realizations provide a prototype for all humanity. . . .

Individual humans doing their own inner healing work. . . .

Oh, *lights* are increasing in number and intensity now! I am watching all humans and animals bond together, bringing joy, comfort, healing, understanding, unconditional *love*, honesty, forgiveness, friendship, loving parenting, compassion into their homes, workplaces, communities and within themselves. . . .

I am seeing a Document called "The Gospel of the Holy Twelve," found in a Buddhist monastery high in the mountains of Tibet. It is an early work brought there by members of the Essene Community, who hide it from the hands of corrupters. One of the legends is played out before me, as a truth for all 'time':

And as Jesus entered into a certain village he saw a young cat which had none to care for her, and she was hungry and cried unto him, and he took her up, and put her inside his garment, and she lay in his bosom.

And when he came into the village he set food and drink before the cat, and she ate and drank, and showed thanks unto him. And he gave her unto one of his disciples, who was a widow, whose name was Lorenza, and she took care of her.

And some of the people said, This man careth for all creatures, are they his brothers and sisters that he should love them? And he said unto them, Verily these are your fellow creatures, of the great Household of God, yea, they are your brethren and sisters, having the same breath of life in the Eternal.

And whosoever careth for one of the least of these, and giveth it to eat and drink in its need, the same doeth it unto me, and whoso willingly suffereth one of these to be in want, and defendeth it not when evilly treated, suffereth the evil as done unto me. . . .[6]

Lights are blazing from all corners of the Universe. It's almost as if cosmic fireworks of initial *Creation* are flaring yet again — in a re-creation! The first brought the physical into being. What I am seeing now is a big bang of *spiralling*

Spirit. Is it the great Sabbath? Let me slow this down because I am witnessing such a stupendous event that I cannot take it all in, and —

Oh, my gosh! There are beings all around me — you won't believe! They also want the scenes to slow down, because we have jumped 'ahead' of ourselves. But, I tell you, what I've seen will make you smile for sure. I am giddy with it all, and I've only seen it in a 'flash'.

These are the *magnificent shifts*. It is the millennium, no doubt. It's the Good News! It is about transcending. 'Past' and 'future' are opposites, and the eternal NOW transcends them. Check your dictionaries. I am talking about going beyond, rising above, knowing no bounds. . . . Um hmm. In this 21st Century 'time,' we are moving to another dimension — going beyond, rising above this 3rd Dimensional reality you have in your hand. You know — the way a work of art transcends paints, canvas and brushes. No. Wait . . . there's more. This process is not simply transcending duality, the illusion of separateness.

No . . . it is ASCENDING. Yes! That's it, ASCENDING! It is not of 'time' and space . . . it is where unlimited growth is possible. It is where *LOVE* exists — because *LOVE* does not exist in a limited 'time/space' box. It is what Buddha terms Nirvana, or Enlightenment . . . what **JESUS** calls the Kingdom of *GOD*, being born of the Spirit . . . it is the Zen's

Satori . . . the Hindu's Self-realization . . . the Moslem Sufis' ma'rifa. . . . It's ALL in front of me!

Yes! Yes! My gosh! Connections are *spiralling*! I see a Sacred Triangle* comprised of the elements of *myth*,* *magic** and *mystery*.* Myth — from stories as they represent 'history' in the making, becoming elevated throughout 'time'. Magic — heightened sense of science as it seeks higher Spiritual realities. Mystery — what still remains behind the veil. As the greater picture is unveiled, I see mysteries revealed which have been Earthly secrets.

Myth, magic, mystery — The Sacred Triangle — the seedling of *Creation* itself as ALL THINGS GREAT AND SMALL connects with *SOURCE!* They become higher *nature*, forming *SOURCE* as it expands into greater dimensionality. ALL THINGS GREAT AND SMALL connects directly to this Sacred Triangle — and **CHRIST CONSCIOUSNESS** is the glue that binds!

I am so amazed! I'm seeing many humans waking up from a long, long 'time' of sleepwalking, and doing their inner work. One cannot be fully conscious and appreciative unless One first wakes up. Ah, but I also see so many clinging to old patterns and fears, exhibiting anger and judgment toward anything that might stir an awakening. I know. I know. Waking up can be painful. But when we are ready, the way is there. The Universe awaits.

And I have learned this: we are new to ourselves each 'moment'. Truth is a constant awakening process. Who I am is fluid. When there is only <u>what is</u> in a given 'moment' — there is peace. Ideals, or what <u>should</u> be, are an escape from NOW. And, usually <u>what is</u>, is a fear of what people will think, of society's 'rules,' of disease, death, dogma, and on and on. . . . In this ASCENDING, there is nothing to fear. NOTHING. We are moving into HARMONY and what we know as the AT-ONE-MENT. It is pure JOY. It is fulfillment of the following ancient writings — I see them lighting up the sky, surrounded by a million shooting stars:

. . . *The lion shall lie down with the calf, and the leopard with the kid, and the wolf with the lamb, and the bear with the ass, and the owl with the dove. And a child shall lead them.*

And none shall hurt or destroy in my holy mountain, for the earth shall be full of the knowledge of the Holy One even as the waters cover the bed of the sea. And in that day I will make again a covenant with the beasts of the earth and the fowls of the air, and the fishes of the sea and with all created things. And I will break the bow and the sword and all the instruments of warfare will I banish from the earth, and will make them to lie down in safety, and to live without fear.[7]

The illusionary view of the world is only what is in the eye of the beholder. As One seeks higher *LOVE*, illusion is lost. As **CHRIST CONSCIOUSNESS** essence is retrieved from within ALL seekers, <u>we</u> indeed <u>become</u> **CHRIST CONSCIOUSNESS ON HIGH**. Earthscape is transformed into what *THE CREATOR* meant it to be: *THE GARDEN OF ALL THINGS GREAT AND SMALL*!*

You know there is no such thing as many-ness: only multitudes of beingness within the UNITY of ALL THINGS. And within ALL THINGS there is only the completion of the bond which encompasses ALL THAT IS. It is only *ONE SPIRALLING DANCE* through the mind — body — spirit: an experience of *Creation*.

It is so. I AM every feeling, every thought . . . every song, every movement. . . . I AM the wolf and the lamb, the clouds and the sea. . . . I AM the fish and fowl, the trees and the mountain. . . . I AM infinity, *light*, *love*. And I . . . AM . . . YOU.

**WELCOME TO 5ᵀᴴ DIMENSION EARTH,
THE PEACEABLE KINGDOM,
THE GARDEN OF ALL THINGS GREAT AND SMALL.
OH, IT <u>IS</u> GLORIOUS!!!**

GLOSSARY

AKASHIC RECORDS: soul level records containing the essence of all history, throughout civilization at large, within eternal manifestation of all higher truth and within every detail of form throughout the greater universes. The Akashics of Old are the messengers of all manifestation throughout history. The Akashics of New are the messengers of unveiling, as secret spaces are opened to planetary evolvement within All Things Great and Small (71).

ALL THERE IS (OR ALL THAT IS): Source On High or God On High (2, 5, 20, 41, 68, 76, 83, 110, 115, 176).

ALL THINGS GREAT AND SMALL: the concept of the God-spoken soul contract between animals and humans within the Interlife period, which states that the finding of higher truth is a shared bond among all Earthly manifestation, that for planetary evolvement to occur, it must occur within all consciousness. Animals and humans are bonded to heal together within the process of global expansion, and animals are here to teach these truths to all who will listen. Christ Consciousness links with this concept in order for it to be achieved (15, 18, 24, 28, 37, 46, 54, 60, 61, 69, 71, 76, 81, 103, 112, 118, 119, 126, 145, 148, 150, 155, 174, 176).

ALTERED STATES: the heightened consciousness achieved through linking with the broader mind (147).

ANGELIC CONSCIOUSNESS: the presence of messengers from the angelic realms, whose emanation is achieved simply through asking (160).

ANIMALSCAPE: the combined essence of all animals as they await higher Godliness to raise the consciousness of greater Earth (11, 19, 35, 43, 60, 61, 76, 109, 112, 122, 126).

ARCTURIAN SISTERHOOD: the Sisterhood from the Star Arcturus which emanates from 16th Dimension and which offers to Earth Goddess Essence, as harbingers (wayshowers) of Christ Consciousness of the Second Coming (78, 81, 118).

AS ABOVE, SO BELOW: a concept which emulates the mirroring of all essence within other essence, as truth is found within all consciousness, and God is present both in elevated form and within the self in the same measure of truth (33, 67, 160).

ASCENSION: the ability of each individual being to move into higher form through inner evolvement and organic change (73, 111, 112, 160).

ATLANTIS: a futuristic civilization which emanates into Earth consciousness as an advanced higher culture (65, 67).

AWAKENING: the unveiling process within each truth seeker, as one opens up to greater realities (102, 147, 156, 166, 175).

BIRDSCAPE: the combined essence of all birds as they await higher Godliness to raise the consciousness of greater Earth (45, 128).

BOOKSCAPE: the essence of the higher book in its Earthly manifestation (72, 117, 164).

CAT NAP: the altered state which takes the cat into realities where it can send healing, or track essence, or shift between dimensions for its own healing (103).

CATSCAPE: the combined essence of all cats as they await higher Godliness to raise the consciousness of greater Earth (103).

CAT SENSE: the cat's higher realities as it seeks love within Earthly existence (100, 102, 104).

CELLULAR RESTRUCTURING: the process of transforming essence at the core level as DNA is transmuted to higher realities, or higher vibratory openings; this is accomplished as one seeks higher truth (68).

CELLULAR STRUCTURE: the essence of a being's internal mechanism at the core level of existence within its DNA structure (14, 103, 118).

CENTER: Source of God On High (3, 6, 7, 17, 20, 77).

CHAKRA: one of multiple energy centers (Sanskrit word meaning wheel of rotating energy) within/without the body where consciousness is experienced and emanates outward and inward.

CHANNELING OF HIGHER SELF: the process of opening up higher co-creative abilities through the clarity of creative imagination, as one expands the inner self through trust and faith. In channeling, one connects with the global higher consciousness of Source.

CHRIST CONSCIOUSNESS: the essence of higher Godliness as it is taken inward and outward into higher truth; the placement of higher truth within the knowing of all created beings (11, 19, 45, 60, 61, 72, 103, 112, 117-119, 126, 145-148, 158, 163, 164, 166, 167, 174, 176).

CHRIST CONSCIOUSNESS OF THE SECOND COMING: the embodiment of the essence of truth seekers, as it rises and elevates to higher Godliness (117).

CIRCLE OF ALL THINGS: the completion of truth within all manifestation as the higher Nature Connection is found (109).

CO-CREATION: humanity's higher ability to manifest form and conceive Earthly existence (39, 76, 79).

CODON: the basic component of DNA structure; out of a potentiality of 64 codons, humans currently utilize 20.

CO-EXISTENCE: the sharing of Earth as our planetary home by all manifestation in equal and high ways (29, 98, 153).

COMMUNICATION HANDICAPPED: the status of greater Earthscape as it awaits the manifestation of higher truth for all beingness (96).

CONSCIOUSNESS: the essence of all manifestation under God (5-7, 10, 11, 13, 15, 16, 19, 20, 29, 31-36, 38, 39, 44-46, 48, 52-55, 58, 60, 61, 64, 66, 67, 69, 72, 76, 97, 98, 100, 103-105, 107, 108, 110, 112, 116-119, 126-130, 134, 135, 138-141, 145-150, 157, 158, 160, 163-167, 170, 174-176).

CORD OF HIGHER TRUTH: the emanation of Christ-like realities into animal essence, through a stream of consciousness found exclusively in Tibetan High Dogs at this time, and whose prototype can be sought for further evolvement within meditation (145).

CREATION: the initial Earthly realization of The Divine Plan, on all levels of higher manifestation, within All Things Great and Small, as the human-animal bond is formed (2, 6, 7, 10-12, 16, 18, 20, 23, 33, 36, 39, 45, 52, 60, 70, 76, 79, 109, 111, 129, 133, 165, 172, 174, 176).

CREATION STORY: the original story which offers Earthscape the truth that all manifestation under God is created in equal realities and common soul essence, as they together seek Source (12).

CRYSTALLINE STRUCTURE: faceted higher consciousness made of Oxygen and Silicon substance, whose source emanates from higher cultures such as Atlantis and Lemuria; crystalline energy is termed "synergy" and its essence transmutes cellular consciousness into higher truth just by being within its presence (2, 66, 68).

DALEIAN CONNECTION: the consciousness which connects interdimensional beingness within the higher realities of global expansion.

DENSITY: the level of bodily consciousness as it elevates to God; density is found at high levels within greater Earth consciousness (8, 12, 13, 17, 21, 23, 75).

DIMENSIONALITY: the existence of vibratory levels within openings to differing regions of consciousness (25, 65, 138, 150, 155, 174):

*3rd Dimension exists on greater Earth for most consciousness (7, 21-23, 30, 78, 80, 96, 99, 104, 105, 134, 142, 157);

*4th Dimension is the healing plane for Earth beingness as it leaves Earth en route to higher truth (157);

*5th Dimension is the higher reality where ascended masters live and wherein the Ascension Process takes one; its essence is higher form within a lighter body than currently found on Earth (159, 176);

DIMENSIONALITY (CONTINUED)

*6th Dimension is where the Elowisian Plane exists for Earthly animals to heal while still in form (104, 105, 138);

*9th Dimension is home to the Pleiadian Sisterhood;

*12th Dimension is home to North Star Sisterhood and the dinosaurs, and its essence is that of light body (9, 17, 45);

*18th Dimension is home to the Arcturian Sisterhood and the dolphin higher essence;

*20th Dimension is home to the Sirian Sisterhood.

DIVINE PLAN: the totality of eternal beingness as it manifests inward and outward within all Creation (72, 102, 119, 130, 132, 154,155).

DNA: molecular structure within all consciousness on Earth, and surrounding Earth itself (67, 103, 137, 158, 163-167).

DOLPHIN PHENOMENON: the communication to Animalscape from the dolphins which happens at a future point when the concept of All Things Great and Small connects at higher and deeper levels with Christ Consciousness; as these messages are also heard by humanity, there results a link among all consciousness for realities of a higher nature (126).

DOLPHINSCAPE: the combined essence of all dolphins in Earthly form as they await higher realities, and as they awaken the higher consciousness of greater Earth (35).

EARTH: a planetary home which contains beings of consciousness, and whose origins are recent within the greater universal picture.

EARTHSCAPE: the combined essence of all consciousness, including humans, animals, minerals and vegetation, as it awaits higher truth (12, 18, 19, 24, 27-29, 31, 40, 44, 48, 49, 51, 96, 97, 122, 127, 129, 132, 133, 143-145, 148, 160, 163, 164, 176).

EARTH SCENE: the greater emanation of All Things Great and Small as it seeks higher realities (48, 60).

ELECTROMAGNETICS: the reconstruction of Earth's grid by Christ Consciousness in order to realign greater consciousness with higher truth (60).

ELEVATOR: a metaphor for the rising consciousness of seekers, and also the means to openings to higher realities (157-159, 165).

ELOWISIAN PLANE: a place of caretaking on the 6th Dimension overseen by Sirian Sister Elowis, where animal consciousness can seek healing as a "safety valve," while the Earthly animal is still in form (49, 55).

END TIME: the turn of the century period of years, leading up to the year 2012, during which global expansion is completed (35, 52, 66).

ENERGETICS: the loss of love as humanity denigrates its connection with Earthscape at large (11).

ENERGY: the essence of individual inner truth as it flows within and without one's consciousness (5, 47, 59, 63, 68, 72, 91, 108, 117, 156).

ENERGY CENTER: one of multiple focal points located within/without the body, where consciousness is experienced and emanates outward and inward; each center may also be known as a Chakra, or wheel of rotating energy (72).

ESSENES: pre-Christian Jews traced back to the Maccabean Age, and described as a unique and virtuous race; translated in Hebrew as "the pure minded," "the holy ones," "the ancient saints or elders," they are referenced in the Dead Sea Scrolls as possibly the lineage of the wise ones of the early ages. Because of their nontraditional and enlightened lifestyles, they are also considered by some to be heretics or fanatics (85, 88, 89, 171).

EXTRATERRESTRIAL SENSE: the deeper understandings by Earth consciousness of forms of a higher order who inhabit Earth but are not visible to greater planetary beingness (129).

FACE ON PLANET MARS: the 20th Century phenomenon formed through Sirian technology in order to elevate and challenge Earth's consciousness of greater realities (53).

Fairyscape: the combined essence of all fairies as they await higher consciousness to acknowledge and embrace their Earthly realities (31).

Form: essence as it appears within the confines of a body, whose purpose is in being a vehicle for the instilling of truth (10, 12, 18-22, 25, 29, 37-40, 47, 51, 65-67, 71, 77, 83, 85, 88, 90, 102, 105, 110, 124-126, 131, 140, 141, 150, 152, 154, 155, 158, 167).

Free Will: the Earthly concept, which exists for all consciousness, of the right to make choices without God's intervention (6, 7, 11, 20, 63, 77, 79-81, 157).

Gaia: the greater Earth scene within all manifestation (121).

Garden (The): The Garden of All Things Great and Small in its higher emanation to Earthscape (1, 2, 47, 48, 159, 169, 176).

Garden of All Things Great and Small: higher Earthscape within 5th Dimension wherein all manifestation seeks Source and Source alone (176).

Garden of Eden: the original garden within the Creation Story of old wherein the link between humans and greater Animalscape was not realized (47, 159).

Global Bonding: the forming of commonality among all Earthscape manifestation in seeking of higher truth (15, 16, 167).

GLOBAL EXPANSION: the evolvement of all Earthly beingness in the common finding of higher truth (15, 52, 108, 118, 150, 151).

GODDESS CULTURES: those civilizations throughout history where all aspects of higher truth have been validated (70).

GODLINESS QUOTIENT: the percentage of Earthly seekers of higher truth (161).

GRANDEUR OF HIGHER ANIMAL SPLENDOR: the essence of Christ beingness in pure form, as viewed from Source (159).

GREATER PLANETARY ZOOLOGICAL ARENA: The Intergalactic Confederation of All Higher Consciousness which exists in form within the greater picture, and includes Amphibia and Tri-lateral beings not known to humanity at this time (150).

GREATER SABBATH: completion of spiritual growth (the universal) within the individual being, as higher truth is realized at levels of physical, mental, emotional and spiritual consciousness (110, 111).

HARSTAL: a greater crystalline structure whose higher truths emanate from Lemuria (2, 64-66, 68).

HEALING OF THE ONE: the concept and technique that healing of one being within a species heightens the entire consciousness of that species (135).

HIGHER SELF: the Essence of God as It emanates into the self within form.

HIGHER SOUL RECORDS: The Akashic Records of Old and New which store all histories of higher manifestation, as they are opened up from the soul level (38, 61).

HOLOGRAM: a sacred shape containing the force of Creation within itself, and holding within its structure the view of all manifestation (6, 21).

HYPNOTHERAPY: a technique which uses the altered state, as it connects to consciousness at all levels, to spiritually heal and learn within the global bonding process (148).

I-CHING: Ancient Chinese classic, also called Book of Changes, which is thought to access the collective unconscious mind and which explains the great riddles of expanding DNA (164, 165).

ILLUSION: veiled consciousness on Earthscape as seen from the unawakened state of mind (20, 26-28, 61, 75, 77, 79, 80, 112, 125, 173, 176).

IMPLANT: the placement of highly focused consciousness internally within a being in order to speed the awakening processes (142).

INSIDE AND OUTSIDE OF CREATION: all levels of elevation to Source throughout spaces which manifest within consciousness everywhere (109).

INTERCONNECTEDNESS: the linking of all manifestation together within one soul (15, 24, 107, 110, 111, 132).

INTERGALACTIC CONFEDERATION OF ALL HIGHER CONSCIOUSNESS: the higher extraterrestrial beingness which exist throughout the greater universes, and which are united in seeking higher truth (118, 150).

INTERLIFE: that period of time between lives, after one's life review, in which the soul is honored for the 'previous' lifetime and in which the next life is planned; soul contracts from 'previous' lives are also assessed within the greater meaning of soul growth (15, 16, 152, 154).

KEEPERS OF THE LIGHT: those seekers of higher truth, both in Earthly form and in light body, who manifest Godliness within their realities (75).

KEEPERS OF THE RECORDS: humans, crystals or animals who store records of higher consciousness for the purpose of greater Earthly dissemination (66).

LAMB OF GOD: the true higher connection between humanity and the greater Animal Kingdom as found within the concept of All Things Great and Small as it connects with Christ Consciousness (146).

LEMURIA: an advanced civilization of the future which seeks the highest manifestation known to humanity, in its embracing the concept of All Things Great and Small (64, 65, 67).

LIFE REVIEW: that period of assessment within the Interlife (the time between lives) when the previous lifetime is reviewed by God for the purpose of validation, learning and healing (16).

LIGHT BODY: form within higher realities, at increased vibratory levels and with less density (157).

LOCH NESS MONSTER: the combined essences of many water beings joined together for protection within Earthscape, seeking higher love through these realities (48).

LORD OF THE DANCE: As purported in Hindu Religion, Shiva, who represents the flow of life, and whose dance keeps the Universe in motion (115).

LORE: Earthly reality as is found within the greater Animalscape wherein density seeks expression at lowest levels of consciousness (49, 96, 98, 131, 133, 150, 152, 153, 157, 161).

LOVE: the highest form of consciousness which can be expressed among and within beingness, and which validates highest truth (5, 8, 10, 12, 14, 17, 20, 21, 23, 27, 28, 33, 35, 38, 43, 48, 49, 55, 60, 63, 66, 67, 73, 77, 80, 85, 87, 90, 95-100, 102, 110, 113, 117, 118, 122, 125, 126, 128, 129, 133, 135, 138, 140-143, 145-147, 152, 153, 157-159, 161, 167, 170-173, 176).

MAGIC: the heightened sense of science as it seeks higher Spiritual realities (33, 57, 138, 156, 174).

MAGNETICS OF EARTH GRIDS: the electrical resonation within its structure that supports greater Earth life (68).

MANIFESTATION: All That Is in form as it emulates its Creator (8, 10, 12, 15, 20, 27, 31, 37, 38, 46, 53, 54, 58, 60, 61, 63, 71, 73, 90, 99, 129, 133, 135, 141, 144, 159).

MELCHIZEDEKS: a higher Earthly body of sacred consciousness embracing seventy two orders, which, aligned with The White Brotherhood, have brought Christ Consciousness into planetary manifestation (116).

MERGING OF CONSCIOUSNESS: interconnectedness between and among species, as dimensions blend and cross over, such that one becomes the other, and vice versa (55, 58).

MYSTERY: that which still remains behind the veil of consciousness (110, 174).

MYTH: elevated stories as they represent "history in the making" (174).

NATURE CONNECTION: the merging of humanity with All Things Great and Small, as the forgotten link is remembered, and global bonding is completed (10, 69).

NATURE KINGDOM: the greater Animalscape as it connects with greater Earthscape (29, 95, 111).

NORTH STAR SISTERHOOD: the constellation from the Star of the Northern Hemispheres which offers Earthscape wisdom gained through higher seeking of planetary evolvement over the millennia. Emanating from 12th Dimension, the Sisterhood specializes in beginnings and endings (8, 9, 18).

ONE HUNDREDTH MONKEY PRINCIPLE: the concept that when a certain critical number (critical mass) achieves an awareness, it may be communicated from mind to mind; and at a certain point, if only one more being tunes into a new awareness, an energy field is strengthened such that this awareness is picked up by almost everyone (137, 156, 157).

OPENING: the space which the seeker creates at the cellular level to connect with one's Divine inner nature (39, 72, 118).

ORIGINAL LANGUAGE: the flowing of all manifestation from Source into Earth as consciousness seeks itself and merges with surrounding consciousness within realities of higher love. Words are not needed because the vibration of sound seeks only what resonates from higher truth (58).

PANORAMA: The Earthly scene before the reader, as it is played out for One (19, 21, 43, 50, 58, 60, 66-68, 75, 88, 89, 110, 111, 121, 163, 169).

PARADISE LOST: The Garden of Eden, as it was meant to be within higher realities.

PEACEABLE KINGDOM: The Garden of All Things Great and Small as Earthscape seeks Oneness within all manifestation (176).

PINEAL GLAND: a small glandular structure in the brain, also called the third eye as it connects to the pituitary gland. Described as the seat of sacred geometry, it was also thought to be the seat of the soul. The key to realignment of the higher energy centers, the pineal gland is activated through the harmonics of sound as well as in meditation; its higher purpose is to enable the return of a forgotten, ancient way of breathing (72).

PLANETARY CONSCIOUSNESS: greater global awareness in the evolvement of higher truth (116).

PLANETARY EVOLVEMENT: the expansion of greater Earthly realities within the seeking of higher truth (10, 12, 15, 16, 39, 40, 69, 70, 159).

PLANETARY EXPANSIONIST: a being who emanates forth consciousness of higher truth (134).

PLEIADIAN SISTERHOOD: The Sisters from the Pleiades Star System who emanate from 9th Dimension and who are here to offer higher realities for planetary evolvement (124).

PROTOTYPE: an image or ideal which can be represented in greater realities and then expanded upon within greater consciousness (145, 156, 171).

REIKI-TYPE HEALING: energetic release and rebalancing within the body's energy centers, as vibratory levels are also raised through the healer's intention (102, 108, 124, 141).

RONAR: God's Top Dog within Animalscape, as representative of higher soul essence which emanates from Source (101, 103-105, 109, 123, 125-129, 131-137, 141, 142, 144, 146, 148, 149, 151, 152, 154-156, 159-161).

ROTATE: the process of inner meditation, journeying within, prayer or soul retrieval (17, 35).

SACRED GEOMETRY: the geometric designs whose essence connect all of life, and within which are contained the seed of life.

SACRED TRIANGLE: the seedling of Creation itself comprising myth, magic and mystery as they become higher nature through connection within all levels of global bonding (174).

SECRET LANGUAGE: the original language or language of the soul, known only to Animalscape at this time (26).

SECRET SPACES: universal energetic cells divinely placed within each Earthly being for expansion of higher truth (13, 14, 17, 45, 46, 103, 128, 131, 135, 142, 148, 157, 158, 160, 165).

SHAMAN: a wise one (25, 90, 115).

SHAMANIC VISIONARY ZOOLOGICAL ELEVATION: the rotation within to finding higher essence through use of animal visualization, for the joint healing of human and animal consciousness (149).

SHIFT: each step along the way in the Ascension Process, as an individual being, or an entire species elevates its consciousness to the next vibratory level (63, 64, 100, 138).

SHIVA: As purported in Hindu Religion, Lord of the Dance, who represents the flow of life, and whose dance keeps the Universe in motion (115).

SIGN: a visible message from higher truth which offers something of benefit to the receiver (130).

SIRIAN CONNECTION: the joining together of higher Earth and Sirius for Earthscape's growth and healing within the global expansion process (52, 122).

SIRIAN SISTERHOOD: The Sisters from Sirius Star who emanate from 20th Dimension and who are here to support Earthscape's higher realities within the global expansion process (52, 150).

SISTERHOOD ON HIGH: the combined Sisterhoods of all planetary existence which are bonded together to support higher Earth's global expansion (20, 110).

SKYSCAPE: the combined essence of the skies and other elevated beingness such as the clouds, stars, and larger atmosphere as they await higher truth (128).

SOUL: the essence of God within each being as it evolves into Higher Self (7, 12, 13, 15, 16, 20, 21, 23-25, 28, 29, 38, 41, 52, 58, 61, 71, 72, 75, 77, 96, 97, 105, 111, 138-142, 148, 152, 154, 155, 157, 158, 163, 164, 166, 167).

SOUL CONTRACT OF SURRENDER: the soul contract unique to Earthly existence whereby the animals surrender beingness to their human connection and wherein reality demands the combined healing of both animals and humans; healing potential is thus taken into the highest risk to form itself, in that if not successful, the form concept is lost to greater civilizations within the higher Divine Plan (154).

SOUL ESSENCE: the substance which comprises the vital inner force of Godliness on all levels of manifestation (23, 25, 29, 140, 155, 164).

SOUL LAW OF DIMINISHING RETURNS: the principle that the loss of higher essence within a species results in a loss of greater soul essence for all Earthly manifestation (29).

SOUL LOSS: the reduction of soul essence at higher levels as a species becomes extinct on Earth (28).

SOUL RETRIEVAL: the process of reinstating lost aspects of the greater self, as it applies to an individual or a species (148, 158, 163, 164).

SPECIESISM: the belief system which places the Nature Kingdom at the lowest hierarchical level of Earthly manifestation (111).

SPIRAL: Described as the golden mean, the spiral is the force within Creation which seeks Center and therein manifests truth within All Things Great and Small (23, 79, 161).

SPIRALLING: the finding of Center by going backward and forward in linear time into the timelessness of Source within the Creation Process; as the spiralling process takes one to Center, it sends all levels of reality into highest truth (2, 6, 7, 19, 21, 76, 110, 116, 127, 140, 172, 174, 176).

SPIRIT GUIDES: beings at the soul level who provide support and guidance for those in Earthly form (26).

STRUCTURAL INTEGRATION: the ability of an individual being to receive higher truth and to incorporate its essence at the cellular level of consciousness (137, 152, 158, 163).

SUBCONSCIOUS MIND: that part of global consciousness accessible through the mind's altered state and which stores, within its records, the answers to personal transformation and evolvement (69, 148).

SUPERCONSCIOUS MIND: that part of global consciousness which connects directly with Higher Self, and which accesses the global mind of God.

SYNERGISTIC EFFECT: the greater results of the combined essence of more than one form of higher truth (107, 128, 149).

TELEPATHY: non-verbal communication between beings such that language is understood within higher form and truth (37, 117, 153, 156, 157).

TRACKING: the abilities of certain animals, such as the cat, to focus on higher realities and to transmute this essence into healing for other Earthly beings (102).

TRANSMUTATION: the changing of inner structures or energetic cells as the individual seeks higher purpose (13, 14, 46, 77, 97, 99, 103, 108, 133, 138, 147, 157).

TREESCAPE: the combined essence of the trees as they await higher Earthly consciousness (31, 109, 128).

TWIN FLAME: the highest soul connection available in form, wherein each twin flame is the same soul essence as the other (2).

VEIL: the essence of illusion as it engulfs the consciousness of each individual on Planet Earth (72, 117, 167, 174).

VIBRATIONAL LEVEL: frequency at which a being rotates into higher essence, as determined in part by intention and in part by Divine Plan (29, 30, 52, 53, 64, 65, 79, 131, 143).

VISIONARY BEING: an individual human or animal who is able to see and emanate higher truth (30).

WAITING FOR GOD: the state of awareness of higher truth (160).

WATCH: the condition of awaiting higher truth on an individual or planetary level (160).

WAYSHOWERS: visionary beings who are able to show higher truth to others; The Arcturian Sisters are wayshowers of Goddess Energies on Earth (75, 118).

WHALESCAPE: the combined essence of all whales in form and at soul level as they await higher Earthly consciousness (59-61).

WHITE BROTHERHOOD: a group of higher beings who represent the Holy Spirit, as they serve to bring to seekers solace, comfort and new learnings (61, 116).

WHITE WHALES: the group of highest whale essence, which stores Earth's historical connections and elevates these records to higher truth (60).

WITHIN AND WITHOUT: the totality of The Divine Plan as it emanates into Earthscape for all consciousness; the oneness of all things.

YEOMEN: the caretakers of planetary consciousness at the soul level (18).

ZONE OF AVOIDANCE: the term given Earth by other planetary consciousness to describe our planet's desolation of higher truth (166).

ENDNOTES

1. From *MAGIC WORDS* by Edward Field, 1968, Harcourt, Inc.

2. *The Gospel of the Holy Twelve*, Lection LXVI, 1-8.

3. *The Gospel of the Holy Twelve*, Lection VI, 18-21.

4. *The Gospel of the Holy Twelve*, Lection XLI, 1-6.

5. Taoist philosopher and Chinese mystic, c. 330 B.C.

6. *Gospel of the Holy Twelve*, Lection XXXIV, 7-10.

7. *Gospel of the Holy Twelve*, Lection VI, 15-16.

ISBN 1552122285-9

9 781552 122853